All Holidays
Volume Two

AN NCPA ANTHOLOGY

A Collection of Fiction and Nonfiction
Holiday Stories
by NCPA Authors and Poets

RoseMary Covington Morgan, M.L. Hamilton, Sharon S Darrow,
Scott Charles, Claire Vogel Camargo, Barbara Young, Elaine
Faber, Frances Fuller, Mike Garner, Ronald Javor, Lorna Griess,
Patricia E. Canterbury, Bobbie Fite, Judith Embree, Jackie
Alcalde Marr, Charlene Johnson, Susan Beth Furst, Denise Lee
Branco, Shelle Renae, Yvonne Whalen, Carolyn Radmanovich,
Bob Irelan, Judith Vaughan, A.K. Buckroth, Christine "Chrissi" L.
Villa, Daniel Schmitt, Norma Jean Thornton, Roberta "Bert"
Davis, Sandra D. Simmer, Barbara Klide

ALL HOLIDAYS: VOLUME TWO

A collection of fiction and nonfiction holiday stories by NCPA writers and poets.

Published by
Samati Press
P.O. Box 214673
Sacramento, CA 95821
www.sharonsdarrow.com

This book is independently published by Samati Press in arrangement with individual members of Northern California Publishers & Authors: www.norcalpa.org.

Printed in the United States of America

ISBN: (paperback) 978-1-949125-33-7
       (ebook) 978-1-949125-34-4

LCCN: 2022908100

Table of Contents

TURNOVER 1
ROSEMARY COVINGTON MORGAN
THE CHRISTMAS MIRACLE.................................. 6
M.L. HAMILTON
REUNION 11
ROSEMARY COVINGTON MORGAN
MOTHER'S DAY SURPRISE.............................. 14
SHARON S DARROW
A MORE PERFECT UNION.............................. 19
SCOTT CHARLES
A GIFT REMEMBERED.................................. 25
CLAIRE VOGEL CAMARGO
SIX TALL SENTINELS 28
SHARON S DARROW
HOW I MET MY FAVORITE SHOES 29
BARBARA YOUNG
HARVEST JACK'S REBELLION 35
ELAINE FABER
3 WATTS ALL AGLOW................................ 39
BARBARA KLIDE
CELEBRATING IN GRIEF.............................. 41
FRANCES FULLER
THE BROKEN TOY 45
MIKE GARNER
JULY 4TH PICNIC 51
SANDRA D. SIMMER
MY ESPECIAL COSTA RICAN HOLIDAY.............. 52
RONALD JAVOR
CHRISTMAS IN MISSOURI.............................. 62
LORNA GRIESS
MAKE TODAY BETTER................................ 65
NORMA JEAN THORNTON
TANNER SULLIVAN, P.I. HALLOWEEN TEA, ILLUSIONS AND......66
PATRICIA E. CANTERBURY
BE MY VALENTINE?.................................. 75
BOBBIE FITE
FROHE WEIHNACHTEN MERRY CHRISTMAS 1959............. 82
JUDITH EMBREE
WHITE CHRISTMAS MORN'.............................. 91
SANDRA D. SIMMER
CINNAMON COFFEE 92
JACKIE ALCALDE MARR
GRANDMA HANNAH'S THANKSGIVING VISIT 102
CHARLENE JOHNSON
THE WAYWARD LEAF 115
NORMA JEAN THORNTON

ANOTHER CHRISTMAS CAROL 116
  SUSAN BETH FURST
GOLFING IN REVERSE 118
  DENISE LEE BRANCO
DANCING LEAVES 122
  SHELLE RENAE
SPLIT SEQUENCE HAIKU 128
  CHRISTINE L. VILLA, SUSAN BETH FURST, & CLAIRE VOGEL
  CAMARGO
SANTA'S MAGICAL VISIT 131
  YVONNE WHALEN
TURKEY WINDSTORM, NOVEMBER 24, 1983 135
  CAROLYN RADMANOVICH
THE SANTA FE SPECIAL & HALLOWEEN MOON 140
  SUSAN BETH FURST
THE MAGIC OF CHRISTMAS EVE 141
  BOB IRELAN
CELEBRATE 146
  JUDITH VAUGHAN
WISHES 151
  SUSAN BETH FURST
A TRADITIONAL POLISH CHRISTMAS 153
  A.K. BUCKROTH
PHILIPPINE DEBUT: A RIGHT OF PASSAGE TO
ADULTHOOD 159
  CHRISTINE "CHRISSI" L. VILLA
A DICKENS' REVIEW 166
  SUSAN BETH FURST
A CHRISTMAS OF CONSEQUENCES 168
  DANIEL SCHMITT
THANKSGIVING MEANS TURKEY, NOT SHRIMP 173
  NORMA JEAN THORNTON
HOLIDAZE...FROM A CAT'S VIEW 185
  KNIGHTLY NACHT, THE CAT & ROBERTA "BERT" DAVIS
THE CHRISTMAS SPIRIT 191
  SANDRA D. SIMMER
PURPLE HEART DAY—MIA 195
  BARBARA KLIDE
NCPA * OUR PURPOSE * WHO WE ARE * WHAT WE DO . 206
OTHER NCPA ANTHOLOGIES 207

TURNOVER
ROSEMARY COVINGTON MORGAN

Parsley, sage, rosemary, thyme and all the other fragrances the song forgot to mention perfumed my kitchen this Thanksgiving morning. Yep, Thanksgiving, my favorite day of all with its earthy aromatics so different from the sugary, cinnamon delights of Christmas or the smokey, fruity breezes of the summer holidays.

I started cooking the day before with my vegetables and desserts, leaving the star of the show for the actual holiday. The turkey, slipped in the oven just at 6 a.m., was having a slow bake until two hours before being served, all golden and juicy. The perfect bird for the perfect day.

I had inherited this day of showcase cooking from my mother, who many years before in an act of unusual suddenness, kicked the stove, banged the counter and said, "No more! I'm sick of this bullshit. You take it from now on!"

I followed her demand and now, with the turkey roasting, sat tired but blissful on the sofa with a cup of coffee and a slice of the secret sweet potato pie I put aside for tasting. I thought the rest of the family was asleep when my almost four-year-old grandson snuggled beside me.

This child represented all that made life precious -- the cutest, smartest, adorable little angel ever gifted from heaven. That is, until...he lifted his beautiful brown eyes to mine and said, "Grandma, why do you look so old?" That was the moment I knew the child was actually hell-sent.

"What makes you think I look old?" I said, sure he would rescue his place in my world with some flattering explanation.

But, no. The hateful little urchin reached upward, touched my chin and said, "Your face, Grandma. Your face looks old." Babies don't lie.

1

Shock! No one had ever called me old. In fact, I was often complimented on my youthful appearance, my great skin, my wonderful smile. I gently pushed the little demon aside and ran to the bathroom mirror to see what he saw. Something terrible must have happened overnight.

Nothing had changed. The reflection I'd seen every day since forever looked back at me. The dark circles and lines around my eyes just meant I hadn't slept well the night before. The little sagging in my neck meant I needed to stand up straighter.

Suddenly, I could hear my mother saying,

"Sit up straight! Don't slouch!" and

"Don't frown at me, girl! Someday your face might get stuck!" and,

"Don't talk so much! You won't have anything to say when you die!"

I never knew what that last statement meant, but it surely had something to do with why I looked old that day.

I picked up my tablet and replaced all the tabs opened to Thanksgiving recipes with photos from my recent class reunion. My husband had said, "Honey, you look better than every other woman here." I remembered feeling smugly pleased. Had he lied? Well, I had graduated early so maybe the time had caught up with me in the intervening months.

I enlarged their pictures to be sure I hadn't missed some youthfulness in my classmates' appearance. Next, I enlarged my pictures and noticed the signs of aging in my neck as well as the circles and wrinkles around my eyes. My aging signs were not much different than those of my classmates. My husband had lied, leaving me to months of aging without my knowing it.

Facebook clued me to something else. All the ads I saw were for old folks' things: solo travel, senior college classes, comfortable shoes, fashions for older women, hairstyles for older women, assisted living, burial plans, cremation sites, and funeral services. Even Facebook is calling me old! Still worse, they seem to be moving me toward the grave. I began thinking censorship might be a good idea.

I started thinking about television ads. Shampoos,

lipsticks, designer clothes, and fragrances no longer grace my screen. I'd become more than familiar with "discreet" adult diapers, arthritis rubs, irritable bowel solutions, and memory enhancers. Someday, with all these aids, I may be able to go comfortably outside for a walk. Knowing how ads are marketed, I vowed to never again watch a police procedural, sitcom, talented everyday people, or stars dancing.

I'm a woman of action. I was not going to have anyone else remark on my oldness. I would stop this enemy from advancing. I googled "anti-aging solutions". There are many.

First was exercise. I checked my gym membership to see if it was still active, and upgraded to a more intense package. I also signed up for a personal trainer.

Next the culprit of the weather. I needed to protect my skin from the sun. I might have to convince my husband to move from the dry, dehydrating furnace of Northern California to the damp, dripping sauna of the southern east coast.

Diet, an important element of continued youthfulness, was high on the list. I filled my online shopping cart with foods I never heard of as well as some I knew but hated. This was no time to be picky. I also doubled up on the foods and spices I already used. I would be eating fatty fish for every meal.

Then there were the creams. There was a cream for everything—eyes, forehead, mouth, neck, hands, hair. The prices ranged from eighteen dollars to over five hundred dollars. I couldn't be cheap with such a critical problem. I decided on an all-purpose cream to fight all my ills. So much for Christmas presents.

Confident I was on the way to a much more youthful appearance, I returned to the kitchen to finish my Thanksgiving preparations. As soon as I opened the oven to check the turkey, I realized the dry heat caused wrinkles. I raised my apron to cover the lower part of my face and put on sunglasses. My family gave me quizzical looks but only my daughter-in-law, the demon child's mother, asked if I was okay. I told her the heat was too hot. Only she wouldn't follow up on such a stupid answer. The other family members were accustomed to my sometimes-unusual behavior.

The turkey was beautiful, even more golden than usual since I forgot it for a bit while I sought anti-aging solutions. Everyone was happy as we settled in for a joyous family evening of wine, board games, and football.

A year later, I was once again in the kitchen preparing Thanksgiving dinner. I don't know if I looked any younger from my anti-aging efforts that lasted until I ran out of cream and got sick of salmon. For sure, I would be avoiding my once again precious grandson this morning. But I invited his mother into the kitchen to help.

My mind turned to Mother cooking in the kitchen of a house with a stained porcelain sink, no double oven, garbage disposal, stand mixer, food processor, or any of my other toys.

She, too, loved Thanksgiving. She sang while she cooked; the only time she sang.

I have often wondered what made my mother kick the stove, pound the counter and give up cooking for Thanksgiving. I thought it was because she was tired but now, I wonder. I am finding little messages have a way of quietly tapping you on the shoulder warning a change is needed. A warning that no cream or diet or exercise can deny. I think I got my first tap last Thanksgiving.

It doesn't always mean age or cooking. It can be anything you do that helps you to recognize the need to step back some. Giving someone else a chance may be hard.

Mother may have gotten her clarifying message on that important Thanksgiving morning and received it with anger and frustration. She lived years after and I never saw her that angry again.

Nor did I hear her sing.

RoseMary Covington Morgan recently left a successful career in transit planning and development to accept a new challenge as an author. She has been writing for almost 3 years.

Since beginning to write, RoseMary has published the short story, *The Song* in the anthology Storytellers-Tales from the Rio Vista Writers' group. She also has 3 short stories, *My Big Red Shadow*, *T'was* and *School Shopping* plus two poems published in the Northern California Publishers & Authors Anthologies.

She has completed one novel and one novella. As of this date only the novella is being considered for publication.

RoseMary currently lives in Sacramento, CA.

THE CHRISTMAS MIRACLE

M.L. HAMILTON

Christmas 1995 arrived with me five months pregnant with my second child, trying to create a Christmas for my oldest boy that he would remember forever. Especially since it would be his last Christmas as an only child.

He was three, so if I'm being honest, the odds of him remembering this Christmas were slim, but the sauce of hormones coursing through my system had me feeling very emotional. It didn't take much to set me off – the commercial where the young man returns home from college and wakes his family up with the smell of fresh brewed coffee; the sight of a puppy bouncing in the grass; the sound of *Amazing Grace* sung by a choir; a magnet of a dove on the refrigerator. Okay, that last one is weird, but come on, *Amazing Grace* – when have you heard that song and not gotten a little weepy?

So, here I was, a week before Christmas, wanting to force as much Christmas cheer into our lives as I could. There's nothing better than the excitement of a little one at Christmas, and Kyler was no exception. Except he was.

See, my first born wasn't like most children. From the time he was a toddler, he would take a toy and turn it upside down to see where the batteries went. He wasn't enamored of stuffed animals or fuzzy blankets. He made *systems* in his bedroom out of a jump rope, plastic blocks, and a toy workbench his grandparents had bought him for his birthday. Kyler adored his grandpa, because he was the only other person who understood Kyler's fascination with mechanical things. Kyler didn't want anyone in his room, besides Grandpa, because he didn't want the rest of us rubes to ruin his system.

When Grandpa asked him what the system did, Kyler regaled him with his theory of *light-tricity*, which as my father puts it, tracked really close to what real electricity does. Who am I to know? I'm as comfortable thinking it's magic as anything else.

All of this backstory boils down to one thing – Kyler loved trains more than anything in the world. For the first ten years of his life, we didn't go on a vacation that didn't involve a train of some kind. He had the wooden train track, and all of the cartoon train characters, but as far as Kyler was concerned, there could never be enough trains in the world.

If anyone had seen what my family and I bought this three-year-old for Christmas, they would have thought we were trying to push him into being a genius. We'd gotten him a child-sized laptop, a talking Teddy bear that read stories (I knew he'd be more fascinated by the mechanics of it, than by any story it might tell), robots and electric cars, and…I kid you not, a fanny pack that he would be able to cover in tools and duct-tape. Once Kyler's father told me he wasn't taking the boy to the store with him anymore because it was too embarrassing to see all the crap the child had hung around his waist, making walking difficult.

Since I was so determined to make this Christmas memorable, we took Kyler to see Santa. I'd been asking Kyler for weeks what he wanted for Christmas, but he kept telling me he didn't know. When the preschool school teacher had them write a list to Santa, I'll admit to a little clandestine spying. I even had my father ask him in one of their confidential meetings about light-tricity. But all Kyler would say is he didn't know.

Santa was my last hope.

As Kyler climbed onto Santa's lap and Santa asked him what he wanted for Christmas, I leaned closer, trying to hear what he said. That is, I leaned closer until a harried teenager *ma'amed* me and asked me to step behind the line because I was getting in the way of her photo. Shesh!

To make matters worse, when Santa prompted Kyler to tell him what he wanted, Kyler cupped his little hand by his mouth and whispered. I couldn't even read his lips.

When he skipped back to me, I took his hand and leaned down.

"What did you tell Santa you wanted for Christmas, baby?" I asked.

Kyler gave me a look that said I certainly wasn't the genius caliber of mother he thought he should have had (I got those looks a lot) and said, "That's a secret. If I tell, it won't come true."

For the rest of the time until Christmas, I tried various methods to get the boy to sing. We wrote a letter to Santa, but Kyler insisted on sealing it in the envelope so I couldn't see it. I asked his teacher if he'd said anything to his friends. I even resorted to grilling Kyler's best friend, our neighbor's three-year-old Morgan, but she was worthless as a confidante.

Finally, I resigned myself to defeat, and figured that since he wasn't coming clean, he'd just have to be happy with what we'd gotten him. I mean, come on, we'd bought a baby laptop for pity's sake.

Christmas morning arrived and the three of us opened our gifts. My parents were coming from San Francisco later in the day for Christmas dinner, so we had the morning to ourselves. Kyler opened all his Santa presents and the presents from his father and me. However, as the pile dwindled, I saw his little face crumpling more and more.

After the final present was opened, great tears began falling down his cheeks.

I cuddled him and said, "Baby, what's wrong?"

He sniffled and said, "I told Santa I wanted a real train set for around the Christmas tree, but he didn't get it for me."

Of course, I started bawling, and I couldn't stop. When his father took him to get dressed, I frantically called my parents and told them what had happened. Without hesitation, they promised to try to find a train before they arrived for dinner.

But it was Christmas Day. Where in the world would they find a train set on Christmas Day? We agreed I would leave the "Santa" paper by the garage with some tape and scissors, and they would do their best.

Hours later, Kyler was playing with his new laptop when my parents arrived. My dad knocked on the door and asked Kyler to come outside. Bewildered, Kyler gave his grandpa his hand. My dad led him down the walkway to the roof of the garage. Resting on the roof was a package in Santa paper.

Grandpa said, "What do you think that is?"

Kyler started jumping up and down. "It's my train. It's my train," he chanted.

"You think so? Do you think it dropped out of Santa's pack?" said Grandpa.

"Sure did!" said Kyler, holding up his little arms.

Grandpa took the package down and handed it to Kyler. Kyler raced into the house, sitting on the couch and tearing at the paper, then he looked up at me, his face alight with the most beatific smile I've ever seen.

"Mama," he said reverently, "I got my train."

When I asked them later how they pulled it off, they told me they'd gone to every store they could think of, but finally they'd tried a pharmacy. A clerk found the last train set they had lying on an empty shelf.

Of course, the whole thing brought me to tears AGAIN. And well, when I think about it, I am so grateful for the *Amazing Grace* of my parents who made a little boy's Christmas "miracle" come true.

In 2010, ML Hamilton made her first New Year's resolution – to get serious about her writing. That same year she found a publisher, Wild Wolf Publications, in England and became a traditionally published author. After five years with Wild Wolf, she decided to venture out on her own into the exciting world of self-publishing. Since that time, she's published 55 novels, written an award-winning screenplay and sold more than 267,000 eBooks.

A full-time schoolteacher and mother of three grown sons, ML carves out time to write in the evenings, weekends and during breaks. Her most popular series, the Peyton Brooks Mysteries, is set in her hometown of San Francisco. The Peyton Brooks Mysteries have been in the top 100 on Amazon for over a year and have reached number 2 in the U.S. and number 1 in the United Kingdom, Australia, and Canada in the Mystery Anthology category.

REUNION

ROSEMARY COVINGTON MORGAN

So here we are my friends
Together yet again
Celebrating a time that seems
But a minute
A hazy dream
That sneaks upon us sometimes
To remind us where we've been.

An innocent time
When tomorrow was another hopeful day
Real life was a dream
And oh, so far away.
A time when little mattered
But chasing happy things

Our youthful joy
Could go off course
Sometimes becoming pain
Whose hurts
We now know
Were minutes spent in vain.

Fun was the word
And fun we had
At all the parties
In our basements, living rooms and gyms
We danced and danced
With carefree abandon
As only the wonderfully young can.

We mashed potatoed and bopped

Cool jerked and watusied
Hitch-hiked and monkeyed
Spinning and dipping
Kicking our heels
Twisting our bodies with unabashed zeal
With complicated moves that today would kill.

The Temptations and the Supremes
Gave us coordination and style
Marvin and James
Taught us soul and how to be bold
With his sexiest voice crooning "Hey Love"
Stevie taught us other things
Things our parents would prefer we not know.

While Aretha was "Running Out of Fools"
Smokey taught us heartbreak and yearning for love
Slow dancing through the "Tracks of Our Tears"
All part of the chorus that
Provided rhythm and beat
To our gyrating hips and spirited feet.

We cheered with loud voices for
Football, baseball, basketball and track
Whether winning or losing
Now looking back
The memory is clear
We were champions
Each and every year.

Great teachers and mentors
Spiritual leaders and friends
Neighbors and even strangers
Too many to name
Prepared us to compete
In the joy and sadness of life's game.

We've come together
To refresh and remember

Those years of our life
So short, yet so important
To every step along the way
Becoming the people
Who are gathered today.

Old pictures consume us
With eyes lost in tears
Recalling vibrant faces
Hopeful smiles
Left hanging mid-air
We bow our heads to honor
Those no longer here.

Let's remember all the happiness
The merriment and delight
And shout out one more cheer
To our past
To our future
And the goal of seeing you
Every next year.

For the Soldan High School
Class of '66

MOTHER'S DAY SURPRISE
SHARON S DARROW

My husband, Stan, and I were enjoying the perfect lazy Sunday morning. He'd gone downstairs for the newspaper, and gotten coffee for himself and a cup of hot chocolate for me. The steaming cups were on our nightstands, just within reach from our pillow nests against the headboard. The different sections of the newspaper were spread out around our pajama covered legs, ready for us to enjoy and share at our leisure.

Stan pointed the remote control at the TV on the dresser against the wall across from the foot of our bed. He flipped through channels until something caught his eye, then resumed looking at the paper, content with the TV noise in the background. We had more channel choices than anyone in the neighborhood since his business was selling and installing satellite systems, the latest thing in entertainment in the late 1980s. He considered it his professional obligation to watch all the time as "research" for the company. It was a nice big color TV too, since it was important for him to monitor and assess the picture quality of the different networks and back feeds at all times. Our TV was a new portable one, which meant it filled the top of the dresser from front to back with just a little bit hanging over, but it weighed way too much for me to move without help.

All of a sudden, I realized there hadn't been any noise from the TV downstairs, which was surprising since our daughters always got up early on weekend mornings to watch their favorite cartoons. "I better check on the girls and see what they're up to," I said, hoping Stan would take a hint since I didn't want to move.

"They're fine. They were playing some kind of game in the living room." He didn't move a muscle toward the edge

14

of the bed. "No need to get up. If they need us, they'll call. And if there's a problem or a fight, they'll start yelling."

Couldn't fault his logic, even if it seemed a bit too casual. Then I heard giggling and uneven footsteps on the stairs. I sat up straighter and leaned to the side so I could see through the door to the hallway at the top of the stairs. Two little heads appeared, one with dark brown hair, and one blonde, both with wide eyes and huge grins.

Uh oh, the blonde, six-year-old Shelley, was holding a tray with a plate of food, while Sheryl, our four-year-old little brunette, carried a full glass of milk.

"Happy Mother's Day, Mommy! We fixed you a surprise." Shelley led the way to the bed, with her sister close on her heels. Shelley plopped the tray on my lap— well, she aimed for my lap and I caught it before everything slipped off the plate. I'd soon pay for those good reflexes!

"Hope you're hungry." Sheryl set the glass of milk on the now-level tray. "We made your favorites ... well, our favorites of stuff we could cook."

I was staring at the plate I'd just saved. Oh, my goodness, I'd never expected a Mother's Day breakfast like this. In shock, I reached for the milk, hoping it would help. Wrong! Apparently pouring the milk was the first thing they'd done, since it was now room temperature. I swallowed, trying hard not to gag or lose the smile that hurt my face.

"Look at this," I said to the two little faces with beatific smiles. "Green peas, toast, hot dog pieces covered with melted cheese, and lots of ketchup in the middle to go with everything." I glanced at Stan, whose smile looked more like a delighted smirk to me. "Wow, you guys made so much. I think there's enough for your daddy, too."

If possible, the girls' smiles got even wider as they looked at Stan. "I'd love to have some, but it wouldn't be right for me to eat any of Mommy's special Mother's Day food. It's all hers."

The little faces swiveled back to me. "Okay, you two can fix a special meal for your daddy on Father's Day." Stan's smirk slipped a bit.

No more stalling. I picked up the fork and poked at the

green mound. Now, I like peas as much as anyone, but prefer either fresh or frozen. These little faded green balls had lost their plump, juicy appearance. Instead, they resembled tiny miniature golf balls, with pock-marked, sunken sides from overcooking in a microwave. I poked one, and watched the fork tine bounce off, sending the pea skittering across the plate. That approach didn't work, so I scooted the fork under four peas and carried them to my mouth.

"Good, aren't they?" Shelley said. "And good for you, too."

I nodded, smashing two tough little orbs with my molars, then swallowing all four like a handful of vitamin pills. "Ummmm," I said. "Yummy. And filling too." No question, that sound from Stan was a muffled snort. Oh man, he'd pay for that later, for sure.

I knew I had to eat at least one more mouthful of peas, but maybe they'd be better with a little ketchup. I looked closer at the plate. I could tell that they'd filled the plate before heating everything in the microwave. The ketchup was brown and dry at the edges, and looked a lot like dried blood. Wet in the middle though, so I forked up a few more peas and dragged them through the ketchup. Room temperature everything, but the tangy sauce helped mask the chewy green balls.

"Try the hot dogs, Mommy," Sheryl said, pointing to a brown lump with a bright yellow band covering the middle, gluing it to the plate. "Hot dog pieces with cheese and ketchup."

The term cheese was used somewhat loosely in our house, since Stan's definition of the word was almost any type, slices or solid mass—as long as it came in a box with the word Velveeta on it. I speared a chunk of hot dog with the fork, but the meat didn't even wiggle when the tines lifted out. The congealed cheese had it locked into place. I smiled at Sheryl, who was watching my every move. "You guys did a good job of melting the cheese on top."

"We had to heat it a couple of times," Shelley chimed in. "But it finally worked."

I nodded, trying to ignore Stan's finger poking me in the side as he kept whispering, "Take a bite, honey, they worked so hard fixing this for you."

So, I did. I took a few bites of everything, even the toast that crumbled into dry bread dust the second I bit into it. As a final sacrifice, I even took another two swallows of the room-temperature milk. The girls accepted my "I'm so full, I cannot take another bite" since I said it with a grin. The smile was real too, because their glorious little faces were worth it. My taste buds might not have appreciated their culinary offerings, but my heart was overflowing after the most unique Mother's Day meal I've ever had.

Sharon Darrow is an entrepreneur, business owner, award winning author, public speaker, and expert in caring for neonatal orphan kittens.

Two of her books are about animal rescue: *Bottlekatz, A Complete Care Guide for Orphan Kittens,* and *Faces of Rescue, Cats, Kittens and Great Danes.* Two are inspirational: a memoir titled *Hindsight to Insight, A Traditional to Metaphysical Memoir,* and *Tom Flynn, Medium & Healer.* Her fifth non-fiction is a training manual about publishing: *Navigating the Publishing Maze, Self-Publishing 101.*

Sharon also writes historical fiction. *She Survives, Strive and Protect,* and *Desperate Choices* are the first three books in the Laura's Dash series, inspired by her maternal grandmother. Sharon firmly believes that life just gets better and richer, the longer you live. Her personal motto is "Find harmony within, then all things are possible." Her website is https://www.sharonsdarrow.com

Her publishing website is https://www.samatipress.com

Email her at sharon@sharonsdarrow.com.

A MORE PERFECT UNION

SCOTT CHARLES

We lived on the edge of a small town, which meant that beyond our house was mostly fields, narrow dirt roads, cow pastures and patches of trees, but not many houses.

The town itself had a main street with places to get supplies, a post office, drug store, the kinds of services a town needed. Most of the streets were paved, but not all. Most everybody who lived in town had running water and electricity. One or two of the older places had an outhouse.

It was a very typical kind of town and the people reflected the kind of normalcy that went with that description.

There was nothing particularly special about it.

We lived on a few acres with a small pasture, a creek, a barn for cows and horses and a corral for the horses to run in. We had chickens and the occasional goat. And of course, we had dogs.

But because we lived on the edge of town, we were allowed to have something that was particularly special. A kind of magical keepsake. I didn't know exactly what it was, but I knew it was important and wonderful.

There was a shed set off away from the other structures. It wasn't very big. It was old but well maintained. It had a lock that secured the double doors and windows on either side but those were shuttered from the inside. It had a shingled roof, an odd thing for a shed in those days.

Inside that small shed was where the magic lived.

I was told to stay away from the shed. It wasn't a stern warning, more like a mild admonition. At first, I had no particular interest in it. But every once in a while, a few men would come out to our little farm in a truck, my father and uncles would open the shed and they would haul out a few boxes, put them in the truck, everybody would laugh, and the men would drive away.

It was the laughing that intrigued me. What was in those boxes that made everybody so happy? The fact that this happened only once a year, in the summer, added to the mystery.

Another really odd thing was the shed had a special name. My father called it "The Magazine," which I found odd because my grandmother would read "Colliers" which she called a magazine, and my father and uncles read "Field and Stream" which was also referred to as a magazine.

Eventually I figured it out. The men, and occasionally a woman or two, would always come on July third. The boxes would be loaded up, everybody would be laughing and a bit giddy, and off they went.

And the next day it was the Fourth of July. There would be all kinds of festivities including games, races, music, animals, and best of all, a parade.

All the towns in our county were so small you couldn't really have a Fourth of July celebration in every town because there would hardly be enough people to be in it, and have enough left over to actually watch it. So, everybody agreed to have the parade and the festivities in our town.

It was huge fun, all day long. I could hardly wait. When the rooster crowed, I would leap out of bed, get my chores done and get ready for the big day.

There was so much to do and see, so many people, and a parade with horses and cowboys, a marching band, wagons and carriages all decorated to celebrate the special day.

Fourth of July! The day that marked that point in time when our country emerged from being a territory to become a nation, governed by a unique set of laws and customs.

There was so much going on that day that I was nearly breathless the whole time. It seemed like a week's worth of fun, or a month's or maybe even a season's worth.

And then the sun would go down, we would all start to unwind and relax, it would gradually get darker and the most marvelous thing would happen.

The fireworks! Starbursts and crackling and booms and bright lights filled the dark sky.

And one year, a year when I had begun the gradual transition from the magical thinking of childhood to the rational mind of an adult, I figured it out. The fireworks I saw in the sky had come from our shed.

I suddenly came to this conclusion when the largest, brightest, loudest and most spectacular display lit up the sky.

I went home that evening with a smile so broad my jaw and cheeks were sore the next day.

After that I was allowed to help with maintaining the shed and its contents. The doors on the shed had to be aligned properly, the padlock and hinges had to be tested, the shutters, the roof, everything had to be kept up, secure, water tight and clean so our precious treasure would stay safe.

I was also allowed to handle the fireworks. The adults would explain to me it was an important responsibility. And I took it that way.

Because fireworks were in the domain of the adults, I had the privilege of being part of the conversations they had. Not all of them at first, but over time more and more often.

It was at that point that my father, uncles, mother, grandmother and older cousins began to treat me differently. More was expected of me and I had to behave accordingly.

One day my father and I were cleaning up the shed, which I also had begun to refer to as "The Magazine," making sure there were no mice or other vermin getting inside, when he explained the significance of the fireworks and the Fourth of July holiday.

He said it had to do with the importance of freedom. We were a free country, he said, and that meant we were allowed to determine how we wanted to live and most importantly each one of us was allowed to find our own destiny. My Father said this with the kind of quiet passion that was usually reserved for solemn occasions.

One year, during the Fourth of July celebration, as we were taking a break from grilling and serving food, he looked up at the sky and said, "A more perfect union." I asked him what that meant and he told me America wasn't perfect, that perfection wasn't what we were celebrating.

He explained that we were celebrating the idea that we could create a more perfect union, we could aspire to become something bigger than just one person, something bigger even than all the people combined. We could become a nation of people who were truly free and we could pass that down to future generations. And each generation would take up the task of perfecting the union.

Later that evening when the fireworks lit up the sky, I felt like those streaming lights and little bright stars meant something more to me than just a fun time. Not just paper packed with gun powder set off for amusement but something deeper. They represented an ideal.

That year it seemed like I became an adult. I still had a few years to go, but I was far beyond being a child. And from that day forward when I did my chores, or went about the business of helping on the farm, I made sure to remember that I was working for freedom. The freedom to determine my own destiny. That I was part of a whole nation of people who were doing that very same thing.

There were moments, sometimes more than a single moment, when I felt the strength and ambition of all those common folk inside my heart, inside the very muscles of my body. A whole nation inside me. Working, striving, creating.

Time wore on. I got older and so did my mother and father, grandparents, uncles, cousins. I took on more of the chores. I went away to school for a while, came back, went away again and came back. One day I went away and stayed away. I had gotten married, and taken a job in a city that wasn't so far away we couldn't visit, but too far away to make it something that could be done without planning.

The old folks passed on. One by one, sometimes a few at a time. My cousins took over managing the family farm. Eventually the shed was cleaned out and the responsibility for managing the fireworks was given to another family.

My wife and I go back there from time-to-time. We take our children. We've been there on the Fourth a few times.

It's not exactly the same as it was. There aren't as many people. But it's still the Fourth of July. Our children are still too young to understand all of what it means, but we tell them it's the birthday of the country, and when those fireworks light up the sky it means we're a nation of freedom.

Someday I'll explain it to them, the same way it was explained to me. In the meantime, we'll just enjoy the parade, the music, and the food.

Scott Charles was born in the Midwest and relocated to Sacramento, California in the 1980s. He lives a happy life with his wife and his dog.

Scott has released a novel, NCPA cover award winner *"The Illustrated Hen,"* which is available on Amazon.com. He is also the author of several plays, including *"Dinners with Augie."* You can see some of his other works on his website at www.libernetics.com

A GIFT REMEMBERED

CLAIRE VOGEL CAMARGO

Riding in the car to Dad's company Christmas party, to my seven-year-old eyes, it looked like a white fairyland outside. Under a wintry white sky, everything was covered with hoarfrost – the flat land, mesquite shrubs, scattered oak tree clusters, and the occasional farm, ranch, or oil field equipment. Cattle huddled in an open covered shed. As the car bumped over a cattle guard, I could see ice covering the barbed wire fence.

The party was in a big room filled with long tables, Christmas decorations, food, and lots of families. Dad, my brother, and I helped Mom carry in some covered dishes of food and set them on one of the tables. A lot of people said "Hi" and "Merry Christmas."

The women gathered around the tables of food at first, arranging them. Dad went to visit a bunch of the men.

Some people sat and talked, while the kids ran around chasing each other, giggling, and looking at presents under a brightly decorated Christmas tree covered with colored lights, ornaments, and silver icicles hanging. I remember when we used to hang those long, narrow silver icicles on all the branches of our tree, making it shimmer in the light. This evening, Christmas carols were playing, and we sang to some of them. It seemed like everyone was happy. Voices got louder as time passed.

Our cousins were at the party, too. I always had a good time being together with them. There was a boy there who I kind of knew. We waved at each other and he came over to say hello, but I was a little shy and didn't really talk a lot. His name was Herschel. I thought he was cute, with his brown hair and eyes, and his friendly smile. He was a little older and taller than I was. He went back to his parents when folks started serving food and sitting down to eat.

I had met Herschel the year before, when he came over to my aunt and uncle's house several times. All of us kids would play in the yard, chasing the puppies or looking under the house for the kittens. He would talk to me, and we would laugh about the animals. I remember giving some bread to a horse at the pasture fence, with my uncle. The horse was a beautiful brown color and nickered to me. Her nose was so soft, it felt like touching hair on warm velvet.

The sounds at the party of people eating, complimenting the food, making conversation, and laughing grew louder, and Christmas music played in the background.

Someone at the front of the room stood up and started talking to all of us – welcoming everybody, thanking us for coming, and making announcements. A few people walked around, giving out candy canes. The exciting part came when Santa started passing out presents. That's when it got really loud, with the kids tearing off wrapping paper, squealing, and asking, "What did you get? What did you get?" Kids began showing off their toys and playing with them.

I got up to get more punch, and look out the window. There were snowflakes floating down, soft and slow. All of a sudden, Hershel walked up, looked out the window with me, commented on the snow, and pulled a little box out of his pocket. He said he wanted to give it to me for Christmas.

Surprised, I opened it. It was a beautiful silver heart ring. My first gift of jewelry from a boy. I loved it. Not long after Christmas, his family moved away and I never saw him again. To this day, I have his delicate little ring and memory in my jewelry box.

silver heart ring
my first gift of jewelry
from a boy

 Claire Vogel Camargo, author of *Iris Opening (2017)*, an ekphrastic poetry collection, has poems in various journals and anthologies. Her awards include a Vancouver Cherry Blossom Haiku Festival 2018 Sakura Award, Runner-up in The Snapshot Press Haiku Calendar Competition 2021 (will feature in *The Haiku Calendar 2022)*, and various poetry society contest awards. A retired nurse, RN, BSN, MSN, she and her husband love his fondue and their dogs. Email: clairdelun@msn.com

SIX TALL SENTINELS

SHARON S DARROW

Six tall sentinels, wrapped in dusty green, standing tall in a
straight line.
Silent, planted firmly in place, only movement a gentle
swaying in the wind.
Decades of service, worthy of admiration and love.
Doing the jobs assigned by God centuries ago,
cleansing the air
shading the dwellings around them
providing a privacy shield
nurturing the wildlife taking refuge within their arms
creating rich soil from their discarded needles
A future of continuing decades of quiet service?

No, tomorrow they die.
Healthy trunks and limbs to be severed and discarded,
Sheltered animals to be terrorized, killed or made
homeless.
What could they have done wrong?
injured a person with dropped limbs?
damaged a vehicle in a storm?
sent roots to uplift a walkway?
cracked the edges of a building foundation?
contracted a disease that made them dangerous?
Was this choice a difficult one made after painful thought?

No, they were thought inconvenient,
Their shapes deemed not as pretty as in their youth,
The animals living in their branches considered of no
value,
And their service and place on the planet meaningless.

HOW I MET MY FAVORITE SHOES
BARBARA YOUNG

I have always been an active, outdoorsy type. I enjoy beach combing, hiking, biking, snorkeling and paddling. Because I prefer warm weather, going bare is my favorite footwear.

My feet like to breathe and experience first-hand the gritty, firm, smooth, moist or squish of the terrain. They are rugged with amazing toe dexterity and proudly cultivated treads on their bottoms. When I moved to the Caribbean, I maximized my barefoot time and simplified my shoes to white strappy sandals, sneakers, fins, and my nursing clogs for work. But one Halloween that changed when I won a costume contest.

As a recent transplant, I enjoyed that 'having fun' was a priority. On this casual and laid-back little island, people also loved to dress up and celebrate. With an average of over two holidays per month honored in the Virgin Islands, I found it amusing that Halloween was a top favorite.

That year, they held the Halloween gala in the ballroom of a local hotel. Because it raised money to benefit the fledgling grass-roots animal rescue and care center, attendees were to come dressed as an animal. Local businesses donated prizes for the many drawings and contests.

The island of Saint John had more phenomenal beaches than places to shop. There were a few boutiques, a thrift and sew shop, pharmacy, hardware and several food and variety markets with liquor and souvenirs. Despite that, Carla and I had collected the items for our costumes within a week, including borrowed, recycled, found, and created items.

A few hours before the party, we met for a small

potluck. I arrived with a salad, cheese and crackers, pineapple gelatin, and a bunch of green costume parts.

Her apartment was tucked in below a huge concrete and wood house on a mountain, mid-island in Susannaberg. Because it was already 'bug-thirty', we had to dine inside the screened studio. As the sun lowered toward the horizon, our view, through the branches of the mango, turpentine and tyre palm trees that surrounded us, was of glowing distant turquoise north shore bays.

Carla knew right away what animal she wanted to be. When it came time to transform, she dressed in the black long-sleeved leotard I loaned her, and her own matching stockings and low-heel pumps. She stuffed black leggings with tissue paper to make a tail, and wired black felt triangles with smaller pink triangles glued on them to a headband for bendable ears. When she blinked, her bright green eyes flashed from within the black felt mask framing them. The finishing touches were easy for her, using eyeliner to draw tufts of fur on her face and a muzzle around the glued-on broom bristle whiskers. Her pretty kitty costume was complete when she painted her nails pink and donned a matching feather boa.

As darkness approached, while in her open-air apartment, we became immersed in the crescendoing nighttime chorus of various frogs and bugs, locally called, 'croakies'. I planned to dress as a croakie frog. Collecting the pieces to make it complete was an adventurous scavenger hunt. It was easy to find and recycle corrugated cardboard into a lily pad to go around my waist and webbed feet that held on around my ankles to conceal my sneakers. I then covered the lily pad with shiny green lamé scraps and glued green foil tinsel-cloth to the feet. Large sheets of yellow tissue paper were fan-folded and bound in the center, edges tattered, then fluffed into a large lily flower that I hot glued onto the lily pad. I couldn't find any paint appropriate for skin, so I added green pigment to a light concealer make-up for my face, neck and arms — my only exposed skin.

Carla painted on, for me, a wide froggy grin with deep red lipstick. I wore a lime green leotard and tights purchased from the variety store and the green socks that Ginger, who owned the thrift shop, found for me. Over this, I added a white open-weave crocheted hippie-style front-tied crop top with long flared sleeves that covered the cuff of the green rubber gardening gloves from the hardware store. The final touch was a gold glittered top hat and oversized cardboard cut-out glasses. Large white Styrofoam eyeballs with green centers sprang from wires in a silly dance in front of the lenses.

As we walked into the party, a gnarly pirate with a pet bat perched on his shoulder, instead of the usual parrot, greeted us as he passed by, but we did not know who he was. The extravagant decorations in the large room included satin ballroom curtains, colored lights and a turning mirrored ceiling ball. Representative of the island's growing stray cat population, many sleek black cats circled in the room and pounced to the musical blend of island reggae, calypso and steel pan.

Many interesting costumes filled the room. We were glad to have already eaten because the enormous rat hanging out by the food tables made it unappealing. The guy wore a pointed rat's nose on his face, clawed fingers, and his thick hair was mangled and teased with debris. Dressed in a dirty, holey ragged shirt and pants with lengths of tattered cloth, vine and dangling chaffed ropes, the costume was the rat's nest. From the left side of the room, the judges watched the lively parade of disguised people which continued through the evening, giving plenty of opportunity to evaluate the costumes for a prize. There was an interesting array of witchy animals, animal skeletons and ghosts, which are called jumbies in the Caribbean.

As Carla and I made our first pass on the runway, she flashed her green eyes and slinked the boa. I jiggled as I danced by to accentuate my dizzying bouncy eyeballs. Some judges were poker-faced. Maybe they were trying to figure out if a frog was an animal. Several laughed when my frog-tongue-like party favor unfurled with a toot. My froggy antics drew more positive feedback during successive flirty passes.

Other contestants included a hilarious, furry party animal, clown fish, dodo bird and island donkey with a hibiscus in its mane.

The spotlight shone on the pretty kitty and me on the dance floor a few times. But a provocative leopard crept into the room and stole the evening. Its artfully painted coat fully camouflaged the body and any scant clothing that might have been underneath.

Excitement sparked as the parade of costumes completed before they announced the winners.

The prizes were exciting – things like free dinners, shopping sprees, a day sail, scuba tank refills, motorboat rentals, beachwear, woven hats and baskets, bottles of wine and Cruzan Rum, jewelry and other amazing things.

The judge asked another who the crazy frog was as I passed by. Then he stood and said there was one more special category winner to announce. The mic squealed and the drone of jubilant voices quieted as she announced, "Best Frog Costume!" All the judges pointed at me.

The winners got to dance and strut in animalistic playfulness amidst an uproarious applause. The party ended as the lights in the room brightened.

What a night. I had never won a costume contest before. I had fun, but I didn't know what I was going to do with my prize — a pair of heavy, clunky-looking, thick-strapped sandals that looked like they were made from tires and Velcro — I even considered returning it thinking that they weren't my style. When I visited the store that donated them, I learned they were a Teva sport sandal, made for all terrain wear, including wading and climbing. They made them for my versatile lifestyle, so I tried them, even though I thought they made my feet look big.

Two weeks later, Carla and I went on a weekend trip to Puerto Rico. I would put them to the test as the only shoe that I would bring.

I wore them as we ferried to Fajardo, drove to San Juan, walked through the forts of the old city, and gambled in the casinos of the new San Juan; even when we dined in restaurants, soaked in Coamo hot springs, and kayaked in the mangroves. I kept them on when we toured Ponce, swam in the bioluminescent bay in La Parguera, combed beaches and waded in tide pools near Aguadilla, and climbed through Camuy cave. I was still wearing them on our plane flight back to Saint John. Whether in a dress, shorts, or a swimsuit, those sandals suited me.

Kermit, the famous Muppet frog, once said it wasn't easy being green. But I had a fantastic Halloween wearing green, like a frog. And, besides my bare feet, those funky amphibious sandals became my favorite shoes.

Barbara Young has contributed short stories to the NCPA Anthologies since 2019 and received a recognition award in 2020 for *On the Porch with Miss Lizzy* in their 2019 anthology. Her character, introduced in the 2020 anthologies, the precocious, wander-lustful and heart-driven nurse, Angie, continues to live her dreams in the Caribbean, and on an adventure in Alaska, in the America's and All Holidays 2021 NCPA Anthologies.

Barbara's nonfiction, children's stories, gift and coffee table books that feature her photography are available via her website byoungboooks.com

HARVEST JACK'S REBELLION

ELAINE FABER

"If I've told you once," Papa Red Warty Thing said. "I've told you a dozen times not to stray so far way. Look at you. You're already at the end of your tendrils and into the road. The tractor is coming. You'll be smashed flatter than a fritter!"

Turning toward his parents, Papa Red Warty Thing and Sweet Sugar Pie, unruly Harvest Jack huffed, "I'd rather be a fritter than bored to death, lying face up in the sun like my cousins, Baby Boo, Wee-be-Little, and Jack-be-Little. They never stray past the first twist in their vines."

Harvest Jack's cousins gasped in horror. Such disrespect! Such defiance! And with Thanksgiving right around the corner. Unheard of in polite Cucurbita Pepo society! They turned away from the disobedient cultivar and buried their tendrils and stem beneath their prickly leaves.

"That child of mine shall be the death of me yet," Sweet Sugar Pie declared. "How does he ever expect to become a Thanksgiving dinner pie acting like that? It's your fault. Your ancestors never looked like the rest of us. They were always rebellious."

Papa Red Warty Thing shivered. "If the lad doesn't change his attitude, he's likely to end up gutted, with an ugly face carved in his skin."

Sweet Sugar Pie waved her sticky leaves in dismay. "Don't even think such a thing. My family has a proud history of becoming harvest pies for the past 72 generations. Grandma Sirius Star would roll over in her mulch if she heard of such a vulgar future for one of our clans. I know that some of the Rock Star and Howden crew across the field plan to be gutted and carved up. Some even look forward to lighted candles stuck where their innards used to be. That's not the future I want for our boy." A drop of morning dew trickled from her stem, down her rounded middle, and plopped into the dirt.

"Now. dear. Don't carry on so. The season isn't over yet. It's just growing pains. I'm sure he'll come to his senses when he matures a bit."

Papa Red Warty Thing was wrong, for by now, Harvest Jack had wandered into the road again and lay directly in the path of the giant tractor grinding its way down the road, swooping up all in its path, and dumping the unfortunate ones into a hopper to be carried off to an uncertain future.

Sweet Sugar Pie shrieked, "It's coming! Beware!"

Harvest Jack heard the engine and turned toward the sound. "*Uh-oh!*" The seeds in his belly shook in terror. Papa Red Warty Thing was right, after all. Jack was about to be crunched into a fritter and there was nothing he could do about it.

A raven swooped down and landed on his stem. "It serves you right for being disrespectful and wandering into the road. Papa Red Warty Thing warned you."

How Harvest Jack wished to be alongside his little, white, cousin Baby-Boo, or cousin Wee-be-Little's tiny, orange body. Their future was assured. They would become cute baby decorations, perched alongside a costumed vampire doll in the middle of a mantle, or maybe in a wheelbarrow surrounded by harvest leaves and acorns and a couple of Rock Star or Howdens. Even his distant cousin Lil' Pumpkemon with his white body and orange stripes might end up on the front porch with his larger cousins.

It appeared that Harvest Jack's future lay directly in the path of the tractor, and he was going to be smashed flat and ground into pulp.

Suddenly, he heard guttural, humanoid sounds reverberating through his stem. Harvest Jack felt himself lifted and then felt the cool earth beneath his bottom. What happened? He was lying just inches from Papa Red Warty Thing and Sweet Sugar Pie. Somehow, he'd escaped the wheels of the tractor and was back in his own row of cultivar cousins. "Oh, Papa Red Warty Thing! You were right,"

Harvest Jack cried. "I'll never disobey again. I promise I'll grow up and become a Harvest dinner pie, but...can I choose which kind of pie I want to be?"

"Of course, you can, my dear," Sweet Sugar Pie cooed, stretching her loving tendrils over her son. "Your great aunt was a pumpkin streusel pie with a gingersnap crust, and your great-grandfather was a pumpkin cheesecake."

"Good! When I grow up, I want to be...let me think! I know just the thing. I want to be a cherry pie!"

Sweet Sugar Pie glared at Papa Red Warty Thing and shook her sticky leaves at him. "I knew this would happen. This nonsense is your fault."

"What's wrong?" Harvest Jack cried. "You said I could choose what kind of harvest pie I wanted to be."

"You can, my dear, but you can't be a cherry pie, because you're a pumpkin," Papa Red Warty Thing patiently explained.

"That's what you think," Sweet Sugar Pie screamed. "According to social media today, if the lad wants to be a cherry pie, then he's a cherry pie!"

"You're to blame, Sweet Sugar Pie. You were always too lenient with the boy. I should never have married someone from the other side of the field!"

 Elaine Faber lives in Northern California with her husband and feline companions. She is a member of Sisters in Crime, Cat Writers Association, and Northern California Publishers and Authors. Her short stories have appeared in national magazines, won multiple awards in various contests, and are featured in multiple anthologies. She leads a critique group in the Sacramento area.

Elaine's novels have won top awards from the 2017, 2018, and 2019 Northern California Publishers and Authors annual contests, and Certificates of Excellence from the 2018 and 2019 Cat Writers' Association.

Elaine is currently working on three fiction novels to be published next year.

Black Cat's Legacy
Black Cat and the Lethal Lawyer
Black Cat and the Accidental Angel
Black Cat and the Secret in Dewey's Diary
Mrs. Odboddy – Hometown Patriot
Mrs. Odboddy Undercover Courier
Mrs. Odboddy And Then There was a Tiger

3 WATTS ALL AGLOW
BARBARA KLIDE

The Festival of Lights called Hanukkah
With waxed candles aflicker, all aglow
A week and a day in the menorah
Sitting quite reverent and straight in a row.

During rededication of the Temple holy
Resanctified, and ornate
A day's cruse of oil amazingly found
And the eternal flame lasted for eight.

Favorite gifts are then given; divine fare is prepared
Braided challah, tzimmes, and roasted veggies all shared
With potato knishes, matzo ball soup, latkes and noodle
kugel
If you need these defined, please don't kvetch, go ask your
Uncle Google.

∞

Time has passed, kids have grown
They returned, to a troubling transition
Change can sometimes be strange
But for this one, the change was their mission.

On a trip to the store, they intended to take
For Hanukkah items, needed
A set of tiny bulbs, I saw on their list
Those, verily, could not go unheeded.

What's this I asked, confused, not amused
As they marched in the store, two resolute humans
From aisle to aisle looking for signs
On a quest for 3 watts of 22 lumens.

With a twist of the wrist the burned-out bulbs were
removed
Clearly flameless and safe, they were swapped
Disconcerted I felt, shocked, and saddened, at worst
This strange change, I refused to adopt.

As I heaved a big sigh, consolation I sought
For waxed candles from so long ago
Consolation I got; latkes just hit the spot
Guess I'll live with 3 watts all aglow.

CELEBRATING IN GRIEF

FRANCES FULLER

When Wayne was dying, we planned a party, not in spite of his dying but because of it.

The truth had become inescapable. Surgery was impossible. Chemo had not worked. The bad numbers were going up. The pain was growing, his body shrinking, and the defibrillator, now irrelevant, had to be turned off, while we tried to grasp the days, running like sand through our fingers.

Our son Tim, far off in Seattle, was determined to come to this little town in the hills and honor his dad in the way he could, with a piano concert. And a small mob of people, scattered around California, wanted one more chance to express love and respect to Dad, Grandpa, Uncle, Teacher, Neighbor, Friend.

The dream of a performance on the grand piano in the town's small concert hall had to be forgotten. The guest of honor would be unable to sit an hour in a straight chair.

We would compromise, do what we could, find a way. We would do it in our home, the big house that Wayne conceived and led us to build.

Circumstance and opportunity chose the fitting day, Memorial Day, 2017.

It took a lot of doing, a lot of hands. Emailing, calling invitations. Driving to airports, meeting family rushing in to help. Renting a piano. Borrowing chairs. Picking up rugs. Moving furniture.

Meanwhile the honoree was either asleep or in pain. Unable to sit anywhere for more than a few minutes, he kept moving from his recliner to the couch to a chair to his bed and back, trying to find relief. When the pain was too much, I would give him a pill and he would slip away. On the night before the big event, I prayed that he would (please, God, for just one day) be alert and comfortable enough to enjoy what we had planned.

The concert was set for three p.m. Fearing that Wayne, the most sociable of men, would exhaust himself before the music began, I had asked the invited guests to arrive no more than fifteen minutes in advance, not an easy thing for some who would drive hours to get there.

The rented baby grand stood in our living room. Folding chairs filled every space—the living room and loft above, the dining area, the solarium, the deck just outside the sliding glass doors.

At one o'clock I gave him a small dose of pain medicine and said that I would wake him in time to dress. At 2:00 I found him on the side of the bed, putting on his concert clothes.

At 2:45 a stream of cars began to arrive, from our small town and surrounding communities, from L.A. with two from Texas, the California valley, the wine country, and the East Bay. Someone went out to supervise parking. Others welcomed guests at the door and helped them locate seats. By 3:00 Wayne, pale and gaunt, was in his big recliner near the piano, positioned so he could see the hands on the keyboard and the guests could see him as well, and more than fifty people filled the chairs, while in the loft a few stood, the better to see.

It was a quiet crowd, attentive, focused on the reason for this moment.

Before he played, Tim stood and addressed these words to his dad: "You may be wondering why today's program is all Beethoven. It's not because I thought a deaf composer was best suited for a partly deaf listener. There was a deadline for this concert, and in a race between pancreatic cancer and my ability to learn music, it wasn't clear who might win. It's a sad time for us as we face losing you; meanwhile the terrible things human beings do to each other intrude into our daily news. Beethoven's music feels especially beautiful at such a time. Not just because it is consoling, though it is consoling. Not just because it gives an outlet to our grief and joy, though it does. It's that his music embodies what is best about us. It portrays our search for what is beautiful and true. It shows us groping our way through uncertainty and knocking our heads against a wall over and over until a door is opened. It explores grief, but celebrates joy. And it's inspiring that a person as lonely and as unhappy as Beethoven gave us such joyous music, music that is full of faith in life."

Tim played first the third movement of *Sonata #29*, the "*Hammerklavier*" followed immediately by parts of *Sonata #21*, the "*Waldstein*." Introducing them, he spoke of the pain, frustration and anger expressed in these pieces and how these matched some of his own feelings. After a brief intermission, he then played *Sonata #32*, Beethoven's last, speaking of the gratitude he finds in the last movement and inviting the audience to hear in its theme the words, "Thank you, Lord…"

For an hour we let the music speak, and everything was there. Our struggle and pain and comfort and joy and gratitude, carried on beautiful sounds, searching, singing, soaring and falling into a long moment of silence.

During the applause Wayne got up to hug his son and me. He had sat in that recliner for nearly two hours, alert to everything, listening to every note and basking in the love that filled the room.

Departing, the guests touched his face and his abundant white hair; they spoke gently, reminded him of happy experiences, held his hands, and just sat, some of them, wordless, absorbing the moment, making it last. In words, gestures, hugs, they said goodbye, they said thanks, they said, some of them, "See you up there."

After most had gone, a granddaughter knelt at his feet holding his hands, while he prayed for her, and her boyfriend watched with tears spilling down his face.

That was Monday; he lived until Friday, now and then weeping and declaring himself the most blessed man in the world.

Frances Fuller, recently a resident of Georgetown, CA, writes out of the overflow of a long, varied life. A child of the depression, she has earned degrees in journalism, English and religious education, traveled extensively, built a publishing house in the Middle East, survived several wars, and written numerous books (some published only in Arabic translation), including the triple award-winning *In Borrowed Houses, a true story of love and faith amidst war in Lebanon.* Meanwhile, she was a wife for 63 years, a Bible teacher, and public speaker while raising three sons and two daughters. She has ten grandchildren and four great grandchildren.

On her ninetieth birthday she wrote the final chapter of her most recent book *Helping Yourself Grow Old, Things I Said to Myself When I Was Almost Ninety.*

THE BROKEN TOY

MIKE GARNER

B illy never knew any of his family. He was left on the door steps of Saint Francis Orphanage when he was only two days old.

Many children were given up for adoption during the great depression by parents who couldn't afford another mouth to feed, and orphanages across the country were packed to capacity with kids of all ages during those hard times. Unfortunately, in the 1930s our country had many children with nowhere to live.

Billy was now 12 and only knew the cold regimented life of Saint Francis. The workers were all kind to the kids, but there was never a feeling of belonging to a family. During the night, just before he fell asleep, Billy wondered what it was like to be loved by a family. He was a good boy; however, he didn't talk much, which prevented him from having very many friends. During his life, Billy didn't receive many hugs or signs of affection from anyone.

He knew the chances of being adopted were not very good at his age. The depression kept most kids from being adopted because people simply didn't have the money. On rare occasions some lucky kid would get picked out by wealthy parents who couldn't have children of their own. It was understood that he and the other kids would likely spend their entire childhood without any family.

On a cold winter night Billy walked to the small town near the orphanage. It was Christmas Eve and most of the workers were already home with their families. It was still early and bed count wasn't until nine o'clock so he knew he wouldn't be missed.

Billy understood the true meaning of Christmas from learning in Sunday school about the birth of Jesus. During the holiday season the children each received one present that was donated by the community.

The kids could always count on a second-hand jacket and some worn out gloves. Even the young children in the orphanage knew that times were hard and no one in their community could afford to buy them presents. Billy had never owned a toy of his own.

The kids never got excited during the holidays. It wasn't because they didn't get any presents. It was because they had no family to share their love with. They all wanted the warmth of a mother's touch and a dad to play catch with.

While walking in the snow-filled street, something caught Billy's eye: a small shiny object in the gutter, inches from the storm drain. He looked down and saw a dime about to be washed away into the dark culvert pipe. A flash of energy swept through his body like a lightning bolt. Billy snatched the dime up just as it was about to disappear.

Now what was he going to do with ten cents? Billy looked up and down each store window covered with decorations and blinking lights, until he saw a tiny toy store at the end of the block.

Once he entered the store Billy knew he wouldn't be able to buy anything with just a dime. The army men were the cheapest toys in the store, but they were fifteen cents each.

It was still nice to look at all the expensive toys on the shelves and imagine playing with them in his mind.

He really liked the shiny new bicycles that were in the middle of the store. Kids at the orphanage didn't own a bicycle of their own but were allowed to ride the old bike that was there.

Billy continued to walk around the store when he noticed a cardboard box sitting in the corner of the room under the stairwell. It was dark, but he could see several old toys inside the dusty box. He asked the old man sweeping the floor if he could look at the toys in the box.

The man, who was the owner of the store, didn't remember the box was even there. He pulled it out from under the staircase and saw it was filled with broken toys.

Each toy had something wrong with it. Either part of a toy was missing or they were damaged in some way. The owner remembered that's why he tucked the box out of sight, because no one wanted to buy broken toys.

Billy didn't care if the toys were broken. To him they were perfect. He felt a strange connection to the misfit toys and thought he had something in common with them. No one wanted a broken toy and no one wanted a twelve-year-old orphan boy named Billy.

He noticed a small yellow duck buried at the bottom of the box. The duck was dirty, had one foot missing, so it couldn't stand. To Billy's surprise the broken toy had a fifteen-cent price written on it, so he asked if he could buy the broken duck for a dime, and finish sweeping the store to make up for the extra five cents. The owner agreed to sell him the broken yellow duck for ten cents, and told Billy he didn't have to sweep the floor because it was getting late and he should be running along.

Billy left the store with his new friend and sat down on the side of the street. As he was sitting there admiring his toy, he saw a broken Popsicle stick in the dirt. Using the stick and a strand of string from his raveled jeans he made an artificial foot for his feathered companion.

He carefully tied the piece of wood to the duck's leg. Now, it had two feet and could stand on its own. Billy was proud of his accomplishment and could now stand his toy up when talking to him.

As Billy walked back to the orphanage, he decided to take a short cut through a small forest. He never had taken that way before and soon found himself lost. It was dark and cold out and he was getting scared. He soon found an old mining cave and went inside to look around. He found a box of wooden matches and built a small fire to keep warm on that Christmas Eve night.

He knew he was going to be in big trouble when he got back to Saint Francis. He would have to do extra work duty for several months for his punishment. Sitting by the fire, holding the duck close to his chest, Billy again thought of how nice it must feel to be with a family on Christmas. He stroked the duck's head and wished for a turkey dinner with all the trimmings.

Billy heard a strange sound from behind a large rock in the cave, and looked behind the rock. He couldn't believe his eyes when there was the biggest turkey dinner he had ever seen. Even a pumpkin pie was sitting on a small table. Billy thought about what had just happened and knew it had to be some kind of a miracle or magic. The last thing he did was make a wish and stroke his feathered friend's head.

He wished for a decorated Christmas tree with hundreds of blinking lights, and looked outside the cave. There was the prettiest tree he had ever seen. The decorations were perfect.

It then occurred to Billy his broken yellow duck must be granting his wishes like the genie in the lamp story. He was at the age where he still believed in magic, and he thought he may only have one wish left. What should his last wish be? He didn't have to think long about it. He stroked his duck's head and made the silent request.

He knew he had better find his way back to the orphanage or they would send out a search party to look for him. It took several hours, but Billy finally found his way back to the large stone building he called home.

As he entered the front doors, he didn't see any of the workers, but thought it was late and everyone was probably asleep. Billy opened his dormitory room door, where fifty kids should be sleeping in their beds. To his surprise the room was completely empty.

Billy started to yell out loud if anyone was there. Sister Teresa came into the room with a strange look on her face. She told Billy a miracle happened that night, and explained that people from all over the state arrived at the orphanage at the same time and adopted every child. Billy smiled and walked away only to find himself sitting alone again.

He looked at his duck in private and said thank you for granting his last wish. His last wish was for all the kids at Saint Francis to be adopted on that special Christmas night.

But no parents showed up for Billy that night; there must be a mistake. He didn't know what he did wrong and began to cry. He was alone when he heard a voice. Billy turned around to be blinded by a bright white light.

The voice that came from the light said it was his time to be with God. Billy was not scared even though he knew he had just died. He then recognized the broken duck was the spirit of Christmas which had granted his wishes.

Billy was at peace with his maker and understood that there was a life after death. A feeling of eternal love filled Billy as he stood in the presence of God.

God must have had other plans for Billy, for he suddenly found himself waking up in his own bedroom on Christmas morning. He now had parents and a big brother for a family. Billy didn't remember anything about ever living in an orphanage and it was as if that never happened in his life. He only had memories of a good childhood and loving parents.

He and his brother opened several presents each, before the family had a big turkey dinner. For a split second, Billy had a flash of the cave in the forest, but the image quickly went away, and he now felt the warm feeling of being loved by a family. He was about to fall asleep when he looked over at his nightstand. There, standing tilted a little to the left, was a dirty old yellow duck with a Popsicle stick as a foot.

The broken toy would be with Billy for the rest of his life. Billy later became a pediatric heart surgeon and saved numerous children's lives. That was his last request from his special friend that he found in that dusty box under a staircase. Some things will never be forgotten.

Mike Garner had a different type career in law enforcement: twenty years in the K-9 unit and Bomb Squad, which is unheard of in any department because of the dangerous work. Being involved in numerous high-speed pursuits and thousands of life and death situations including three separate shootings, doesn't even start to tell what he went through as a street cop.

After retiring, he found playing golf didn't satisfy his burning desire to help people in some way. Sadly, he saw the relationship between the police and the public in our country rapidly eroding.

In an attempt to have purpose in life, Mike wrote a book about the things he experienced during his exciting career.

He vividly describes the good and bad things he saw in the line of duty. The public has never heard a true cop story like his. Mike's career was filled with things movies are made from.

Mike's intention is that his book will give a better insight to people on what some cops go through during their careers.

JULY 4TH PICNIC

SANDRA D. SIMMER

Checkered plaids thrown
On the ground host
Sandwiches and chips.
Cut fruit drips tasty juice
Down sundrenched arms.
Potato salad and fried chicken
Might join the picnic fare.
Lemonade or sodas
Satisfy our thirst.

Lazy conversations
Carried by the breeze
Shared under bright umbrellas
Protection from the harshest rays.
Energetic children, with
Bare feet and brown arms,
Fly colorful kites or chase
The family dog around
The park while
Parents rest in ease.

As the sun sets
Low into the horizon,
Families gather together
To lean against each other
And stare in gleeful awe
At the annual fireworks display.
Bright bursts of light put
The perfect punctuation on
Another July 4th holiday.
Memories to cherish for a lifetime

MY *ESPECIAL* COSTA RICAN HOLIDAY

RONALD JAVOR

Holidays and celebrations occur for many reasons. Some take place on a specific day of the year, others celebrate the birth of someone famous, and many are established by laws or traditions to celebrate specific events. In addition, a few happen to celebrate an achievement of a significant specific event. This story is about that last type of holiday.

It was 4:30 in the morning in June 1998 and I was sitting in front of my temporary home in San José, Costa Rica, when a dilapidated pickup truck pulled over to give me a ride.

"Buenos días, Rolando. ¿Como está?" I called out to the driver when he stopped the truck next to me.

Rolando reached over and opened the passenger door for me to slide in. As I climbed in, he said, "Good morning, Ron, please we talk English so I practice better. OK?"

"Sí!" I answered, and then corrected myself, "Yes, English for you! Are we ready to find some wood?" Rolando's request was good for me too because my knowledge of Spanish was limited to important questions like "*¿Dónde está el baño?*" (Where is the bathroom?), answers when asked if I speak Spanish like "*Muy un poquito*" (Very little.), and important pleas such as "*Tengo hambre!*" (I'm hungry!).

This was my second week in San José, and I was working with a local small humanitarian *fundación* (a nonprofit organization) established to help many Nicaraguan widows and children of men who died during the recent civil war in Nicaragua. They had fled to Costa Rica to avoid poverty and further persecution. Unfortunately, they were impoverished as well as being dark-skinned indigenous Native Americans who often spoke little Spanish. As a result, they were not welcome in Costa Rica either, and were offered no assistance or services by the government or government-supported nonprofits such as Habitat for Humanity. Without that assistance they suffered from hunger, homelessness, illness and other deprivations as well as often abusive menial employment conditions and treatment.

This humanitarian nonprofit group spent many months with little success trying to assimilate these refugees into existing affordable housing programs and employment training opportunities. Later, the nonprofit decided the only option was to find land and build, for what we would call a shantytown—shelter from the elements with running water and primitive hygiene.

The group was not able to raise enough money to buy land, but the government finally donated several barren acres of property isolated from transportation and human services, but near electric and water sources. This allowed the group to plan and start construction of this small shantytown community, which also would incorporate supportive services for medical and employment assistance.

The next step was finding money to pay for labor and materials to build the houses. So far, the little money raised merely covered the cost of extending plumbing and electricity to the home sites and purchasing construction equipment plus some specialized materials. As a result, most building materials had to be donated, and the homeless women and volunteers helped design and build the two-room homes on each lot. The men with trucks visited other construction sites each day and virtually begged for donated materials.

The program's organization was simple but effective. We would build on Tuesdays through Saturdays, with Saturday being the busiest day, when those women who did have work elsewhere, could work on the project. Sundays were for church or rest, and Mondays were set aside for shopping or dealing with appointments and other personal needs.

Those women who were physically able worked by digging, building, and carrying supplies. Others, who were older or not physically able, provided support such as childcare or cooking food for the workers. The families from both categories with the most hours worked were entitled to receive new homes and all were expected to continue to help even after they received their own homes. Two homes with their colorful backyard latrines already were completed, but progress had been frustratingly slow because of the lack of skilled carpenters and inadequate supplies of lumber and other construction materials for walls, roofs, windows, and flooring.

The shortage of skilled workers was addressed by recruiting a few volunteers like me from other countries who had construction skills. They also found several local disabled or retired craftsmen who donated some time to the effort. However, limited fund-raising success continued to stymie the ability to move ahead with the construction of more homes. After I arrived, I joined with others, soliciting donations from construction sites.

A surprising solution to the problem of a scarcity of building supplies was provided by a local builder who suggested that instead of driving around to multiple building sites each day and all day long asking for small donations of extra materials, we should go to construction sites early in the mornings before trash pick-ups or the arrival of other scavengers and salvage discarded materials. We immediately discovered this was both efficient and effective, and on the first two mornings we collected significant amounts of what we needed for our simple structures. That is why I was on the street early that third morning before breakfast, leaving with Rolando and his old truck for our morning "dump run."

At our first stop that morning we hit a jackpot: not only large piles of discarded long 2"x4" and 4"x4" lumber, but also unused roofing supplies, a couple of slightly damaged doors, and even many sheets of various sizes of plywood. Several partially empty boxes of nails lay near the trash piles, so we assumed these were available as well. We put on our gloves and loaded the truck until it could carry no more. At that point, the first laborers began to arrive to work and we decided to *vámanos* before we got into trouble.

We made a quick stop for *desayuno* (breakfast) and devoured *los huevos y las salchichas y el café* (eggs and sausage and coffee) with fresh tortillas, and thirty minutes later we were welcomed back at the home site as heroes. We unloaded the truck near the lots for the next two homes, and soon another truck arrived with more materials that we also unloaded.

Normally, at that time in the morning, someone would drive me to my Spanish immersion school so I could learn to speak with, and understand, my new friends. However, we were so excited about all our new supplies, and that we might finish a new home sooner than expected, I stayed and started to supervise and help with construction.

By the end of that day's work, we had built the four outer wall frames flat on the ground; they would be raised the next day onto the wood frame foundation and then nailed together with cross-beams. We prepared the lumber for the cross-beams and surveyed our remaining materials. We decided we really needed more plywood and some type of roof coverings, so the truck drivers were tasked with trying to find those items the next morning—and to pick up anything else of value they found.

At that point late in the day, all the children were returning from school. The mothers prepared snacks for them and the volunteers. Then, while the volunteers played *futbal* (soccer) with the children, work stopped for the day and the mothers prepared dinners for all of us. Afterwards, I was dropped off at my temporary home for a quick shower, a description of the day's events for my hosts, and early bedtime.

The next morning began the same way. We found several residential construction sites which had piles of materials we needed. A few extra sheets of plywood were stacked near the trash piles and we loaded those too. After shopping at a hardware store to buy tar paper and metal straps we required that day, Rolando dropped me off at the language school.

Today the teacher focused, for my benefit, on construction terms, although these terms would be useful for my other classmates as well. We learned words and phrases like "*el martillo y los clavos*" (hammer and nails) and "*el taladro*" (drill) and simple sentences like "*Traeme un grande tornillo por favor*" (Bring me a large screw, please).

After I returned that afternoon to the work site, we had both successes and problems. The first thing we did was raise the framed walls and tie them together with cross-beams. This required measuring, sawing, nailing, and some screwing. I was on a ladder for what seemed to be an eternity that day, using my newly learned Spanish, or just with hand motions giving instructions, to the five inexperienced women working with me. By late afternoon, the walls were up and sturdy, and a roof frame was started.

The problems? A lot of my Spanish left much to be desired and resulted in some confusing or humorous problems during construction. For example, once I asked for a "*martiro to echar un clavo*" thinking I was asking for a *martillo* (hammer) to pound in a *clavo* (nail), but instead, in apparent Costa Rican slang, I had asked for a martyr to make love to. The five women just gaped at me in surprise, then one whispered something to the others. They all started laughing uproariously. The problem: not only didn't I know what was so funny, but I was still standing on top of the ladder holding several pieces of wood together and getting tired. Eventually, one of the women brought what I needed, and I finished hammering and climbed down. Then another woman blushingly told me what I really had said. After another round of laughter, we got back to work and I thought I had conquered that vocabulary for the future.

Two days later, by the end of the day on Saturday, the walls of the first new home were covered with tar paper and plywood on the outside, the roof was started, and the window openings had screens but no glass. Also, the plumbing and an electrical line were ready outside the home. Finally, the backyard outhouse pit was partly dug, but the outhouse itself still had to be built. We would need to find a lot more materials each morning during the following week just to finish our first house.

My Sunday-Monday "weekends" generally were free time to explore Costa Rica. The people here were friendly— although the drivers and roads are terrible—and this was the first country to champion environmental consciousness, placing over a quarter of its land area in nature preserves. The Pacific side is lush and comfortable for tourists, and the Caribbean side is more rustic. One unique aspect of Costa Rica is that there is no standing army; in addition, most of the police don't even wear guns when on patrol or responding to crime calls.

I traveled by bus on two-and three-day trips to many interesting places. One weekend I climbed Mount Arenal, an active volcano, where I felt the earth shaking, smelled belched sulfur, and wondered what it would be like if the volcano erupted (it actually did erupt on my last night in Costa Rica); the second day I hiked through densely forested canyons and relaxed at Tabacon Hot Springs whose pools are heated directly by the volcano.

Another weekend was spent touring several coffee plantations, seeing how coffee was picked and treated, and attending local arts and crafts fairs where beautiful woodwork and jewelry was both sold and worked on in front of customers. I also visited Tortuguero Island, a turtle and tortoise preserve on the Caribbean coast; paddled on a two-day white water rafting trip spanning about half the width of the narrow part of Costa Rica; and spent a relaxing weekend on a beach and horseback riding in Punta Descartes on the far northwestern Pacific edge of the country.

The Costa Rica travel highlight though was Monteverde and the Santa Elena Cloud Forest Reserve. This was the most amazing nature preserve I had ever seen. Everything was green, birds were everywhere, signs of human habitation were limited to a few areas, and the only sounds I heard were birds and the clop-clop of horses available for riding. I crossed rickety rope-and-wood bridges, hiked with bird-watchers in remote areas, visited a butterfly and hummingbird preserve, and generally felt like I was "back to nature." I spent two nights in a hostel's tiny private room for $15 American each night, including dinner and a bag lunch for the next day.

I also enjoyed San José's urban delights some weekdays and nights. I attended a trial in a unique format: the defendant stands or sits in front of the judges (three, not one) and the defense and prosecution are on the side. They ask the presiding judge to ask questions, and the defendant or witness has to look at the judges as they answer.

Most Thursday nights I went to a local college student bar to socialize with local students in English so they could improve their language skills. It also was a karaoke bar and one night, when my resistance was down, I was persuaded to sing Neil Diamond's "Sweet Caroline" — in Spanish, of course — as a duet with a local *senorita*. Never again!

Despite these enjoyable weekends and evenings, it always was exciting to get back each Tuesday to building the homes. We spent the week, following the partial construction of our first home, collecting salvage items and finishing it: completing the roof and covering it with tarpaper, adding plywood and sheetrock inside, building an interior wall and doorway, installing a kitchen sink and adding the front and back doors.

Thinking I finally had the "hammer, nail" vernacular down pat, I helped put in the last finishing connections on the outhouse door hardware. In my best Spanish, I confidently and proudly asked for a *clavel* and a *marído*.

Everybody laughed because instead of asking for a nail and hammer, I said, "Can I have a carnation and a husband?" Sigh.

Our final steps on Friday and Saturday were adding front and back doors, making sure plumbing and electrical worked, scouring the city and our cached supplies for used furniture and beds, and painting the inside and outside of the structure. Of course, at the same time, others completed and painted the outhouse.

Now it was time for the celebration! The *fundación* staff chose the family who would live there, and we announced a "ribbon-cutting" ceremony by them was necessary. Of course, the only "ribbon" available was toilet paper, but we festooned both the front door of the home and the outhouse door with it. Then the mother and her three young children gaily sliced the door decorations open and entered their new home. The group declared Monday would be a holiday, a *fiesta* to celebrate the completion of this home and the continuing work on the next two.

What a holiday! When I arrived at noon, there were rows of *ollas* (pots) and *bochas* (bowls) set up on makeshift tables. In addition to a variety of fruit and vegetable *ensaladas* (salads), there were *pastelitos* (Nicaraguan meat pies), *enchiladas* and *tamales*, *churrasco* (grilled beef), *pollo Mambo* (marinated barbequed chicken) and *rondon caribeño* (Caribbean fish stew), to name a few dishes. All were served with *arroz* (rice), fresh homemade tortillas, *frijoles refritos* (refried beans), or *maduros* (fried plantains). To spice them, there was the national salsa, *pico de gallo* (chopped tomatoes, onions, chili peppers, cilantro, lime juice and salt) or *salsa de frijoles negros* (black bean salsa).

Dozens of women and children—both current participants and hopeful future residents—were there, dressed in their colorful native clothing. They were excited and happy, although many must have had to cook all night to prepare all these foods! We were given tours of the new home, already decorated by its family, and we ate the prepared foods and desserts until we were stuffed. After dinner, guitars and other instruments were brought out and both adults and children entertained all the families and volunteers with music, dancing, songs, and stories. In one story, they even mangled Spanish, pretending they were me.

For the adults there, no holiday *fiesta* is complete without some local alcoholic beverages and these became available after the children went to bed. I think the national drink is *Caipirinha Tica* made with Cacique Guaro (a Costa Rican slightly sweet sugar cane liquor), lemon juice, brown sugar, and crushed ice. Another regional favorite is *Chiliguaro*, a combination of Cacique Guaro, tomato juice, a splash of lime juice and a shot or three (depending on one's taste and tolerance) of Tabasco sauce. At midnight, all the visitors were offered mats and blankets so we didn't have to leave and sleep elsewhere.

After this twelve-hour holiday and what seemed a very short night of sleep, we were awakened abruptly and early the next morning by young singing voices: "*¡Despierta, despierta! ¡Ve a trabajar!*" ("Wake up, wake up! Go to work!"). Then, laughing, they ran away.

I sat up groggily, both remembering the fun we all had the day before and wanting more sleep. Eventually I was up and about, and after a cup of strong black Costa Rican coffee, I could think clearly again. Although yesterday's holiday was over, I was sure that after the next two homes were completed, another holiday would take place. There was still room for about 75 more homes, and definitely the time and desire for who knew how many other holidays, even after I had left Costa Rica.

Ronald Javor lives in Sacramento and spent his legal career assisting people with low incomes, disabilities and homelessness to access safe and affordable housing. Since "retirement", Ron volunteers his time continuing the same work as well as advocating for environmental justice. He also continues his writing interspersed with travel abroad and camping.

Ron has written seven children's books on young people confronting and overcoming these barriers. Each book addresses negative stereotypes and shows that all children, despite their handicaps, have the same goals and desires. His recently-published Young Adult book, *Our Forever Home*, features Lonesome George, the extinct Galapagos tortoise, and Dodo, an extinct bird, exploring the past and present worlds of extinct animals now living in *Our Forever Home*, the effects of climate change, and what can be done about climate change to save today's animals, including humans. More information is available on his books at ronaldjavorbooks.com

CHRISTMAS IN MISSOURI

LORNA GRIESS

One Christmas many years ago, I was an Army nurse stationed at Fort Leonard Wood in Southern Missouri. I had not been home to California for a couple of years so I made the decision to go home for Christmas that year. That was it, all decided, I was going home for Christmas. I called my family. They were pleased. I started to get excited, sang Christmas songs, danced around the house, told my neighbors, requested leave from work, bought plane tickets, arranged a ride to the small airport on post, and so forth. Fort Leonard Wood had its own airport for commuter trips to the nearest big airport.

I had a month to go before my big trip. Friends would ask, "What are you doing for Christmas? You are welcome to have dinner with us."

I would answer, "Thank you but I am going home to California for Christmas this year."

The days crept by slowly, December 23rd was finally here. My plane left in the morning of the 24th. I was excited, had Christmas gifts ready and suitcase packed. I went to bed early and awoke in the early morning hours to a snowstorm.

Not just any snowstorm. This was the worst in recent years, with wind pushing the drifts around covering everything—feet of snow piled up. The forecast showed snow through Christmas Eve and into Christmas Day.

As the day moved on, traffic was at a standstill, flights were cancelled, snowplows fought an endless battle with the piles of white stuff.

I was not going anywhere soon.

I called my parents and cancelled the trip. I stoked up the fireplace to stay warm. The cat crawled onto my lap and we watched the news. What to do? Clearly, nothing.

Christmas Day looked about the same. I started thinking about where to spend Christmas. Calling one of the friends who invited me was an option, but which one would I choose? Then a thought drifted through my mind.

There was a Veteran's Home around here somewhere. I looked it up and it was not far away. I called and cleared the way for a visit. It was afternoon by now. I got in the car and slipped and slid my way to the nursing home. The staff showed me to the nicely decorated dayroom.

I saw one elderly, sad looking man seated at one of the tables, his crutches propped up against the table, and I asked if I could join him. He nodded hesitantly and I sat down. I introduced myself and told him about my situation to start the conversation.

He smiled and told me a little about himself: where he served, where he was from, etc. Before long two more veterans appeared to join the conversation and tell war stories. Then another, and another, until we had men pulling chairs from other tables all over the room. I looked around at the crowd of wheelchairs, crutches, missing limbs, and loneliness and I thought, what a great evening!

Everyone had a war story or a joke to share. The stories of heroism, families, disappointments and joy poured out in floods. Finally, it was dark and I had to leave before the roads iced up.

One man admired the Good Shepherd pendant I had on a chain around my neck. From the look in his eyes, it meant something real to him, so I took it off and offered it to him, and he gratefully accepted it.

I hope those veterans enjoyed the day as much as I did. This day was a gift of friendship, if even for a little while. There have been many more Christmases since, but I will remember this one forever.

 A second-generation native Californian, Lorna graduated from high school and nursing school in Sacramento. Her first job was staff nurse at the Woodland Clinic, in Woodland. Restless, she joined the Navy Nurse Corps with an assignment in Newport RI, just in time for the Cuban Crisis in the early 60s. After two years she returned to civilian life and moved to New York City because the World's Fair was coming. She found a job at Cornell Medical Center on the east side of Manhattan. Missing military life, and with the escalation of the conflict in Vietnam, she rejoined the military, this time, the Army Nurse Corps with a guaranteed assignment to Vietnam. She found a home.

The Army became a career. After serving in a MASH unit in Vietnam, her assignments took her to Germany and all parts of this country. She worked her way through Staff nurse, head nurse jobs in intensive care and oncology. Then had supervisory roles in large hospitals. She retired after 28+ years of service as a full colonel, Chief, Department of Nursing at Letterman Army Medical Center on the Presidio in San Francisco. The hospital closed shortly after she retired in 1990.

Retirement opened up a new world of opportunities. She was a Veterans Advocate at the state capitol for nine years representing The Military Officer's Association. A lifelong hobby photographer, she became an artist. Painting with oils she now looks for pictures to paint in her large stash of old photographs. She has written a book about her year in Vietnam in a MASH Unit called *MASH Vietnam*. She now stays busy with volunteer work.

MAKE TODAY BETTER

NORMA JEAN THORNTON

What kind of things could make today better?
Find in a drawer, that missing love letter

Sweet words from your spouse or significant other
Or words of wisdom from your father or mother

You know your kids listen to what *you* say
When *your* words from *them*, you hear put into play

Your grandkids finally have jobs and are healthy
Maybe one day they might even be wealthy

From a great granddaughter, a kiss on the cheek
Or to hear her squeals as she plays hide and seek

To watch a great grandson, with a gleam in his eye
As he longingly looks at that last piece of pie

Laugh at your dog as he runs after a ball
Or chases his tail all the way down the hall

Spy on your cat as she stalks a bird
And tries really hard, not to be heard

Thanks to all your family and pets, each a friend
Your day is made better from hugs that they send
NJT

Best Friends Day: includes Family and Pets

TANNER SULLIVAN, P.I.
HALLOWEEN TEA, ILLUSIONS AND...
PATRICIA E. CANTERBURY

PROLOGUE

My name is Tanner Sullivan. I was born in the Northern California town of Weed, the great grandson of one of the largest landowners in the county, Liam Sullivan.

Great Grandfather Sullivan arrived in California in the late 1820s as a ship's mate from Ireland along with his Senegalese wife and young son, my grandfather. It is family legend as to how the three of them ended up in Weed, but I do know that great grandfather worked in the gold mines alongside Chinese laborers while great grandmother cooked and made clothes for the few other women in the area.

After many years, my great grandparents were able to buy larger and larger parcels of land on which to raise cattle and a few sheep. Great Grandmother spoke her native Senegalese Wolof, French, and English while her husband, Liam, spoke English, Gaelic and basic Mandarin and Cantonese, which he learned from the Chinese workers. As a result, Grandfather Walter was very fluent in the languages needed for bargaining with early Californians. He even learned to barter in Spanish.

As their holdings grew, so did their influence in the area. My father, Walter Amir Sullivan, became a banker and his older brother, Liam Patrick Sullivan, Jr., became the owner of the family's vast ranch.

I was expected to follow in my father's footsteps and take over the family bank once I returned from a grand tour of Europe after graduation from Stanford, Class of 1925, with my degree in economics.

The Great War had ended and was fast becoming a distant memory, especially for those of us in college. I was on the tour, without a care in the world, when my 16 year old niece, Anna, and her best friend, Li Wang, went missing in San Francisco while on a visit to Li's grandmother. A month passed before I learned the girls were missing. I vowed to find them, and bring them back home.

It's been nearly five years now. I got a private investigator's license so I could work closely with the police, and the fact my family had quite a bit of money helped open doors which normally would be closed to a *colored* man. During the years in which I've been searching various nooks and crannies of the numerous levels of San Francisco's Chinatown, I have been involved in some interesting cases. The following is one of my favorites as it has led to many more cases.

* * *

It was a typical Autumn afternoon. The weather had been in the mid 40s for most of the week. I had been invited to a pre-opening and a Halloween party at the *Sleepy Fox*, the new blues joint right off Market Street. Even though I didn't care that much for the blues, I knew that almost everyone in San Francisco was going to be there and I hoped to gather some information about my beloved niece's disappearance.

Someone told me a colored girl and an oriental girl were seen wandering around the *Sleepy Fox* a week ago, near midnight. The source of my information was not very reliable, and he waited nearly 12 hours before saying anything. I'd been tracking useless clues about Anna and Li's disappearances for years so I was used to folks taking their time to inform me of anything about them. Besides, neither Anna or Li Wang would be considered girls anymore as they both should be close to twenty.

I felt sure that Tommy Sung, the current leader of the most notorious Tong gang in the Bay Area, had them kidnapped and shipped off to some faraway place most folks had never heard of, but I continued my search.

"Hey Tanner, you in your office?" a loud male voice yelled from the front door of my outer office.

"Yeah, I'm here." I replied, refilling the hot water pot for my third cup of *Monkey Picked tea* and adding a shot of gin to smooth my nerves. I'd been up late trying to deal with folks whose days begin after dark.

In walked Raymond Peterson, my roommate from Stanford whom I hadn't seen since we disembarked from the tanker, Viking Princess, a few years ago.

"My goodness Ray what a surprise. What are you doing here in San Francisco?" I walked over and gave him a bear hug.

"I've heard all about the wonderful Halloween parties you folks give in this great city and decided to indulge myself. Read somewhere where you opened a P.I. office. How's it going? Mind if I have a cup of that tea you have there? You know you got me drinking the stuff in college."

Ray pulled up the client's-chair, took off his bulky gray wool coat and picked up a clean cup from the shelf behind him, all the while speaking as if we had just completed a conversation seconds before.

"I just added a spot of gin in mine," I said. "You want it plain or do you still insist on putting lemon in yours?" I teased with the ease we had with each other when we were in college.

"Gin? Where's one get gin nowadays? Prohibition is raging down in Fresno. Have to be on the look-out for Johnny Law."

"Prohibition??? Never heard of it." I replied with a smile while pulling out my gin bottle and putting a few drops in Ray's tea.

"So, you still looking for your cousin...what's her name?"

"Yep. Actually, she's my niece. Not a sign anywhere. I have folks spread out all over Chinatown. That was where she and her best friend were last seen."

"Seems to me a *colored* girl should be easy to find in Chinatown. Especially one who speaks the language. Have you tried having someone infiltrate some of the Tong gangs? I read in the Fresno papers that the Tongs are very, very active up here. Hey, this tea is great. Much better than the stuff I get back home. What's this called?" Ray asked, draining his cup and refilling it with hot water, fresh tea leaves and a thimble of gin. He still had the run-on sentence speech he had in college. If one wanted to ask a question of him, one just had to talk over him, which is exactly what I did.

"It's called *Monkey Picked*."

"Monkey Picked? What an odd name."

"No, it's very accurate because the leaves are from the very top of a special tree where baby monkeys pick leaves and throw them down to the farmer for gathering. The babies weigh between one and one and a half pounds, so they're able to climb high into the branches where the freshest, tastiest leaves are. Only a few Oriental stores barter with non-Chinese to sell the leaves. I'm fortunate to be on their list. I'll get you a package before you leave. Speaking of leaving, how long are you going to be in the city?"

"I plan on taking the first train heading down the valley on November 2."

"Do you have a hotel room?" I asked, hoping Ray would say no and he would be able to spend the next few days with me. "I have a two-bedroom home right off Clay."

"Hotel? No, I was hoping to stay with you. Maybe bring you luck in searching for your niece."

"I could use a fresh set of eyes."

The rest of the day was spent getting Ray settled into my home and buying extra groceries. We ended up having lunch at the Golden Dragon, the restaurant owned by the family of my secretary, Sally.

Fully stuffed with Canton chicken, steamed rice and fresh vegetables, we went to the *Sleepy Fox*, where a band was practicing for the next day's grand opening.

"Tanner, did you follow up on the info I gave you about seeing your cousin over in Colma?" Marvin Jarvis slurred, drunk already before 2 in the afternoon; he had settled into a comfortable booth just inside the *Sleepy Fox's* entrance. It would probably be where anyone would find him if he weren't sprawled in the city jail.

"My niece? No, Marvin, I haven't had a chance to drive all the way there just on who you may have seen over a week ago. But thanks for the information. I will check it out," I replied, pulling Ray by his coat sleeve, not introducing him to the city's famous drunk.

"Tanner, Colma?" Ray said softly. "That's where my mother's buried. If it's really not too far, perhaps we could drive over there and I could place some flowers on her grave." We walked across the dance floor to the other side of the *Sleepy Fox* where the round tables were set up. It would be at least six hours before folks would be arriving for the pre-celebration.

"No, it's really not that far by car, about ten miles or so. We can take mine down there later this afternoon. We should have enough sunlight to find your mom's grave without any trouble, and I can look around to see if, for once, old Marvin might have seen something. Although how he could get to Colma and back is beyond me."

After getting Ray settled in the guest room and filling my car up with gas, I returned to my office to find nothing much had changed while Ray and I were getting reacquainted. Sally had been in and typed up some correspondence, cleaned up the teapot and tea cups, and left me a note that she and her new best friend, Brezy, my accountant's new secretary, would be at the motion pictures if I needed her. As usual, Sally didn't say which motion picture house, but I knew it would be the one where Anna Mae Wong was starring in the latest Charlie Chan mystery.

The drive to the Colma cemetery was slow and Ray asked about the new bridge which was being built across the western side of San Francisco; supposedly I should be able to see a bridge tower from the roof of my office building. We were driving in the opposite direction from the bridge construction, past fields and hills with dying wild flowers and scattered homes clinging to small mounds of dirt pretending to be hills. The fog had already rolled in, making our trip slower than I planned.

We arrived at the cemetery and easily found Ray's mother's grave. I left him alone and walked a few rows away toward a large mausoleum surrounded by a three-foot high iron fence. I turned toward where Ray's mother was buried in time to see him walking slowly toward me, his head still bowed as if in prayer.

As he got close to the iron fence gate both of us heard what sounded like a soft whisper of something in Mandarin. We turned toward the mausoleum and noticed the large, iron doors were slightly open. We climbed over the fence and pushed open the doors further, but didn't hear anything more.

"Anna, Li are you there?" I yelled, feeling very foolish. As if two girls, no, two young women, would be hiding inside a cemetery vault. "It's just the wind," I said aloud more to myself than to Ray.

The leaves rustled near our feet, and the fog rolled in, closing out everything but the mausoleum and us. We walked deeper into the vault, surprised there were little to no spiderwebs inside. In fact, the place looked like it had been freshly cleaned. I hadn't thought to bring the flashlight from the car, so instead, flicked my pipe lighter on just in time to see steep steps right near my toe.

"Careful, Ray, there are steps here in the back."

"Where could they lead?" he asked.

"I have no idea. But I'm going to follow them just in case the noise wasn't our imagination, or the wind."

The steps led down a circular path deep underground, with a hand rope secured to rings sunk into the brick wall under the vault. After many minutes in which we lost track of time and direction, we felt the wind, smelled sea water, and stepped down onto sand just outside a cave a few feet above the rising tide. In the distance we saw what looked like a motorboat, with four people in it, racing over the waves toward the outline of what appeared to be a small tanker almost to the horizon.

The wind nearly blew out my flame, but not before I noticed two sets of small footprints which appeared to be racing toward the ocean followed by two larger shoe prints right behind them. The waves were rapidly washing both sets of prints away.

"Tanner, do you think the small prints may have belonged to your niece and her friend?" Ray shouted above the roar of the waves and the sound of the motorboat.

Returning quickly to the cave and slowly making our way up the stairs where we could talk, I answered Ray's question when we could hear each other: "Why would they be running away? I think this cemetery, the fog, and it being so near Halloween, that we're just wishing we could finally find the girls after all this time.

"I imagine seeing them together almost every time someone mentions the possibility of seeing them anywhere near Chinatown or the port. Maybe we should find out more information from Marvin." We made our way back to the vault and outside to the cemetery, and I continued, as Ray and I hopped into my car and returned to San Francisco. "Let's go back to the *Sleepy Fox,* I'm sure Marvin is still there."

By the time we arrived home, changed and returned to the *Sleepy Fox*, the joint was filled. I had to drive around the block several times in order to find a parking place, which is unusual as I have a spot in the garage across the street. But someone was parked in my space.

"Seen Marvin since this afternoon?" I asked as soon as we were inside. My question was answered by shakes of the head, questioned responses, and shrugged shoulders. The place was full of smoke, loud music, and folks intent on having a good time; the whereabouts of an old drunk was not foremost on their minds.

The *Sleepy Fox* wouldn't officially open until the next day, but it appeared that nearly all of San Francisco wanted to be seen at the pre-opening. It was not an event Marvin would voluntarily miss because even with Prohibition in full swing someone somewhere would have an extra glass or two of whiskey they'd be willing to share.

No one remembered seeing Marvin leave but his booth was filled by a young woman of expensive taste, and an entourage of college boys from Berkeley, Stanford and San Francisco State who hung around, lighting her cigarettes, offering her drinks, which she ignored, and dancing with her from when we arrived to when we left.

The following day I asked around all of Marvin's old haunts, but it looked like he too had disappeared. I even checked with the coroner after looking into the folks in the city jail.

Ray and I checked out the ship listings over breakfast. Both the columns for arriving and departing ships listed for the past week were only passenger vessels no tankers. We must have imagined the boat on the horizon.

"Well, Ray, how about we celebrate Halloween at the *Sleepy Fox* and our getting back in touch? I'll continue to look around for Marvin just to make sure he's okay," I said, as Ray and I got dressed in our costumes for a night of fun.

I never did get to ask Marvin any further questions, because he had disappeared from San Francisco. As far as I know I'm the only one searching for him. It's nearly Halloween a year later, and no word of Anna, Li or Marvin. On the bright side, Ray invited me down to Fresno for Thanksgiving; it will be nice to see him again.

Patricia E. (Pat) Canterbury is a native Sacramentan, political scientist, art collector, retired state administrator, author of seven novels and a world traveler.

Her Young Adult novel, *The Case of the Bent Spoke*, won Honorable Mention at the 2019 NCPA Awards. Pat's short stories have appeared in over 30 anthologies, including the 2018 Brom Stoker finalist, *Sycorax's Daughters.*

Pat and her elderly cat live in Sacramento. Website www.patmyst.com email: patmyst@aol.com

The Busboy's Secret due August 2021 in Obsidian Anthology
A Day in Havana in Destination World, Volume 2 NCPA Anthology
Omens, Medicine Men and Myths in Destination World, Volume 1 NCPA Anthology
The Case of the Bent Spoke A Poplar Cove Mystery 2019 NCPA Young Adult Honorable Mention
Sycorax's Daughter's 2018 Brom Stoker finalist—Anthology
The Geaha Incident an Afro-Futuristic mystery
The Secret of Morton's End, A Poplar Cove Mystery
Carlotta's Secret, A Delta Mystery, Option for a motion picture

BE MY VALENTINE?

BOBBIE FITE

J ill ran a comb through her short brown curls and smiled at her reflection in the little mirror she kept in her desk drawer. She liked the new haircut that showed off, instead of trying to hide, the flashes of silver, and she didn't mind the reminder of her forty-odd years. She checked her watch, applied a touch of lipstick, straightened her suit jacket, picked up her purse, tucked her laptop into the side pocket of her briefcase, and headed out of the office. Nothing could dim the glow she felt, not even the knowledge that by the end of the week she would be hard pressed to finish the ugly report she'd just dropped in her briefcase. After all, today was Valentine's Day. It was her favorite day of the year, and her kids had promised to bake a red velvet cake and decorate it with hearts.

She hummed a little tune as she walked lightly down the hall to await the elevator, tapping her freshly manicured fingernails on the side of her briefcase in time to the tune in her head. Her mind on the dance steps to go with the music, she started to swing into the elevator as soon as the doors opened, and crashed directly into a broad, masculine chest. Her quick apology was drowned out by the clatter of her briefcase hitting the floor, its contents flying in every direction.

This was not how she hoped to start the evening. With a sigh of dismay, Jill dropped to her knees, checked that the laptop was safe, and began collecting her scattered report pages, pens, pencils, and what-not. She checked her watch again as the elevator doors slid closed behind her.

"I'm sorry. Please let me help," a deep voice said. Jill looked up for the first time. She couldn't help but smile. Bending down to kneel beside her was the man with the broad, masculine chest. In attractive addition, he had nearly black hair, straight and soft, with a touch of gray at the temple, and a neatly trimmed beard. His face showed lines of pleasant aging where smiles would be at home. His eyes were a dark, velvet brown. His shoulders filled the jacket of his dark blue suit beautifully. Since her five-feet four-inches had run into him at about mid-chest, she estimated his height as something over six feet. She tried to tone down her smile.

"Wait. Didn't I see you at the party at Joe and Sandy's the other night?" she asked.

"I thought you looked familiar," he replied. "Jill, right?"

"You remembered!" She suppressed a giggle.

He shook his head with what looked like an embarrassed smile and handed her back the notepad from her briefcase. Her name was printed across the top next to a picture of her three kids. "Nice looking family. Which one is Tony?"

"The oldest..." They'd only spoken briefly at the party and she didn't remember talking about her kids. Then she saw the grin tug at the corner of his mouth. "Okay, give it back."

He held up the small needlepoint canvas with Tony's name on it that she had been working on during her lunch break.

"He goes off to college in the fall," she said, "and each dorm room has a place for a name tag. He'll probably hate it, but at least it doesn't have flowers on it."

He handed her the canvas, stood and held out his hand to help her back to her feet. "My name is Tom Bellotti, by the way."

When she placed her hand in his, he asked, "Where were you off to in such a hurry?" He nodded back toward the closed elevator doors.

"Not in a hurry, just not paying attention," she said.

The song she had been humming immediately popped back into her head, and she felt herself blush. *Stuck in Love* by the Judds was not a song she wanted to discuss. *I wasn't looking for mister right; I was looking for mister right now...*

She took a breath and smiled brightly. "Headed home for dinner," she said.

"Have dinner with me instead."

"No, I..." Jill shook her head, shrugging her shoulders in indecision.

"I insist," he said. She had been right about the smile lines around his eyes. "As an apology for nearly running you down."

"I nearly ran *you* down," she replied, knowing there were probably a thousand reasons to say no to his offer, but he had a way about him, this man. A way that made her comfortable right from the start. And he was the friend of her friends. "Well. Okay," she replied. "Thank you. Dinner sounds good."

"Will Tony miss you? The other two kids?"

He was apparently giving her a chance to admit to commitments elsewhere. She wasn't wearing a wedding ring, and she had been quick to notice, neither was he.

"I doubt it. I'll give him a call," she said as she dug her cell phone out of her purse. "He's good at ordering pizza."

"Sounds like my son. With as much pepperoni, sausage, salami and cheese as can be crammed on top."

She nodded and stepped away to make the quick call. When she turned back, he pushed the elevator button and smiled down at her while they waited for the doors to open. It was the smile, she decided. The combination of delight and sincerity in his smile quickened her heart and made her want to change the words of the song in her head from finding Mister Right Now to finding Mister Right.

They left their briefcases in Tom's car and walked three blocks to a small restaurant that served delicious Italian pasta, and had a tiny dance floor. The two-man band played the type of music that you could only dance to if you kept your partner in your arms. Would he ask her to dance, she wondered?

He did, but not until after he'd held out her chair, poured her a glass of rich, red wine, ordered them the house specialty, and listened to her. It was amazing how many married or long-time couples had lost the ability to listen.

She had certainly been there, dashing through the daily routines, taking kids here, off to the job there, solving one family or household crisis after another, plus doing all the general maintenance work of life from laundry to shopping to dinners and whatnot.

Tom took the time to ask about her family. How was Tony liking his senior year of high school? How was Jenny doing in the math class that had made her cry the first day of school? And Alex, how had that little guy talked the music director into letting him play sousaphone in the junior high school marching band? What a treat to listen and be listened to without interruption, except by the waiter serving them.

Through dinner, Jill learned why Tom found his job both fulfilling and challenging. She talked about the people in her office and how they supported each other both on the job and off. She admitted that needlepoint was not her favorite hobby, but she couldn't really run home to dig in her garden during her lunch break. Tom dreamed of travel to far-away places once the demands of family and work were behind him, but in the meantime, he loved spending a weekend here and there, exploring the abundance of history and culture nearby, with maybe the occasional stay in a cozy bed and breakfast.

Jill shared that dream and that love of adventure. When dessert was over and Tom asked her to dance, she realized that in just one evening Tom had been able to capture her heart and soul. It was as simple and complicated as that. She allowed herself to be drawn into the comfort of his arms, rested her head against his shoulder, and felt again the thrill of young love.

"I have a question for you," Tom whispered in her ear as the band played *Everything* by Michael Bublé.

She leaned back to see his face and raised an eyebrow.

He sang along with the music, "*In this crazy life, and through these crazy times, it's you…you're everything.*" His voice was soft, warm, inviting, exciting. Her breath caught in her throat. He paused to smile. "Will you be my Valentine?"

Jill knew that her own smile glowed, that her eyes must

sparkle with the love she felt for this man. "Yes," she replied.

"Good," he whispered. "Will you join me in the hotel across the street?

"Yes. Wait? What did you say?"

"You just agreed, didn't you?"

"That was sneaky."

"But I got the right answer." He leaned forward and kissed the tip of her nose. "I've booked the honeymoon suite, and there's a bottle of champagne on ice just waiting for us. Shall we go?"

"Humm. The honeymoon suite?" she asked.

"And champagne. Strawberries? Breakfast in bed?" Tom said. "It seemed appropriate for our twentieth anniversary. Don't you agree?"

The look on his face was irresistible. She laughed. No wonder she had said the very same word—yes—twenty years ago when he'd asked her to marry him. And every year thereafter, on their anniversary, when they would meet again as strangers, enjoy the delights of a first date, and renew the attraction that had brought them together so completely that whatever question he asked, she would always answer, yes. She said it again this time. "Yes."

Tom reached into his pocket and brought out their wedding bands. He raised her hand to his lips, then slipped the freshly polished, beautiful and cherished ring back onto her finger. She looked at it for a moment, every part of her being humming in harmony with this lovely man, then she lifted her eyes to his.

"Thank you," she said, placing his ring back on his finger. "And the hotel sounds more comfortable than last year's adventure," she added, "although it was kind of fun to snuggle up in the new car and watch the lights of the city come on."

Tom placed her jacket around her shoulders and laughed. "Mostly it was cold. If you'll remember, we had to open the windows because the heater in that fancy new car wouldn't work and the windows were all steamed up."

"Oh, I remember." She tucked her arm into his. "Shall we go?"

"Of course, my darling Valentine."

"By the way," she asked, "how long did you have to wait in the elevator to ambush me like that?"

"Let's just say, our anniversary celebration won't come as a surprise to any of the people in your office."

Bobbie Fite lives outside of Sacramento, California. This is her third story to appear in an NCPA Anthology. She also has three novels. In her first, Lauren's *Nightmares* may be more than just bad dreams. She could be witnessing actual crimes. What happens if the murderer finds out she's helping the police? In her historical novel, *Sunshine and the Bounty Hunter*, the title character has a bright smile, but no memory of her past or why she was riding across the Wyoming prairie alone. Was she riding for help, running away or after something else entirely? Finally, *Storm Damage* takes place two days before Christmas when the roof of a busy shopping mall collapses. Buried in the debris are a young widow, a frustrated cop, a displaced great-grandmother and an abandoned child. They could wait for rescue, but buried with them is a killer with a great deal to lose. For more visit Bobbie's website: www.bobbiefite.com.

FROHE WEIHNACHTEN
MERRY CHRISTMAS 1959
JUDITH EMBREE

So how did I end up here and now?
Once upon a time in a land far, far away there was a fair young maiden and a tall handsome young man…
Isn't that how all fairy tales begin?

Well, this is sort of a fairy tale as well. There we were, two kids in Alameda high school, who started dating, moved on to Cal (University of California, Berkeley), and married in 1955 while Ted was still in dental school at UCSF.

Upon his graduation and successfully passing the State Boards licensing him as a dentist, he was offered the option of entering the military and receiving an overseas posting.

Enlist for two years and you got your choice of countries, but if you had a spouse/child they traveled and lived at your expense.

Enlist for three years and it was an "an all-expense paid" posting. With a wife, one child and another on the way, there was no real question. Three years it was!

Moving forward a few months, which included basic training, packing our few worldly goods and finding temporary housing in Germany (until a unit in military housing was available), it seemed that suddenly there we were. We were experiencing the opportunity of a lifetime, living in post war Europe with abundant travel options just waiting for us. Our busy and full lives continued and two years later, two more children later and then … it was December 3, 1959.

* * *

I was getting excited just thinking of the weeks ahead,

only three weeks to Christmas. It would be the baby's first and the two older girls were almost old enough to feel the spirit and fervor of the season.

Standing in the living room of our tidy apartment I was contemplating the perfect spot for the Christmas tree, and a safe place for the creche, where little hands couldn't accidentally create a disaster. Suddenly the front door opened, the only door to the outside. A jolt of anxiety whizzed through me--no one but my husband had a key. And there he was, a look of resignation on his suddenly tired face.

"Dad died this morning."

Oh no, not that dear sweet man who had always been my biggest fan. Ted's tight voice introduced the gentleman who followed closely behind him. The Red Cross had been notified of the passing and had contacted the Army somehow and here he was to facilitate my husband's return to the United States.

What?

It was, and maybe still is, the role of the Red Cross to notify service personnel of deaths and other disasters "back home" when they were stationed overseas, in this instance Mannheim, Germany. It all happened so quickly and with no discussion with me about logistics, he was to return home today, this afternoon, now!

A bag was quickly packed with a disparate combination of clothes, incidentals thrown in with little thought to how long he'd be gone or what he would need. Time was of the essence, his flight out of Frankfurt was just a few hours away but he had to get there first. All arrangements were in place, he just had to get the bag, get into the waiting car and leave.

There were quick hugs, kisses for the kids, "I'll let you know......", tears and then in a flurry he was gone. And there I stood, in the middle of the living room where just moments ago I was having happy daydreams of a beautiful Christmas.

Reality sunk in quickly. There were baths to be given, mouths to be fed, stories to be read and then, then what? I was so alone. Home, that other "home" more of place and time than people, was thousands of miles away. Family, that other "family" of parents and friends seemed so remote, and of course they were. This year of 1959 held no instant communication through cell phones, Facebook or FaceTime, no messaging, no zoom gatherings, no computers with email. There was the old land line telephone with exorbitant per-minute charges. Why hadn't anyone called to tell us that Dad had died?

An unanswerable question.

Alone.

And yet, not really alone. I had three sweet little beings with me, Leslie at four months, Kristen at 21 months and "big sister" Karen who was a few months short of four years old. Babies, they were all babies.

What I really needed was another adult. I was only twenty-four and so far away from the usual support systems of family and friends. But I did have some of that as I was soon to learn and depend upon.

Letters and other mail arrived through the APO and were delivered dutifully every day by one or two of the enlisted men who worked for "Ted", Captain Edward H. Maxwell, DDS. These young men were so doting, they even offered to help with the girls. I'd imagine they too were feeling the nostalgia of Christmases past, of being far from home and loved ones during the holidays.

The enormity of the responsibility for my three babies and myself was beginning to sink in. I looked around our military quarters, the building itself was a three-story rectangular block with two stairwells each holding the doors to six apartments. This was our second location on Post. We were fortunate enough to have three bedrooms, one bath (tub, no shower), living/dining room combination, and a small but efficient kitchen.

Military housing reflects "spare and basic" as one could expect, but it was very low cost, warm in the winter, and just so-so in the heat of summer. Air conditioning was not something I would expect, having lived in the San Francisco Bay Area almost all my life. I was used to opening windows for "air".

The military issue furniture was truly basic; however, we had just recently taken delivery of several pieces of beautiful Danish modern teak furniture, that was reflective of our taste for sleek design, warm natural finish wood and woven wool fabric of saturated jewel tones. So now the living/dining rooms looked more like home. All we needed was the Christmas tree.

Christmas in Europe is celebrated very differently than in the U.S. There still are *Weihnachtsmarkte* (Christmas Markets) held, such as the one in Heidelberg, near where we lived and, incidentally, where both Kristen and Leslie were born at the U. S. Army Hospital. The Christmas Markets are redolent with aromas of grog (mulled wine), roasting chestnuts and candied almonds cooked in huge copper kettles, and cinnamon and cardamom from stollen (Christmas bread made of an egg rich dough and studded with sweet candied fruits).

Oh, my what lovely sights and smells, and then there were the many beautiful handmade gift options, from delicate lace to sturdy wooden toys, hand-painted metal ornaments, and clip-on candle holders for the "purest" tree decorators. We used the clip-ons one time about four years later; that tree was magnificent, all glowing with candles. Clearly a fire hazard and not to be tried on a dry tree! It was set up near the front door and we even had a small fire extinguisher handy. As though that would douse a tree fire! But we were still young and had to try a candle-lit tree at least once.

All that cold snowy December of 1959 there were very few outings, no car seats for kids and only a rickety little carrier for the baby. I had one foldup "umbrella" stroller, so Kristen would be in that, Leslie in my arms, and Karen holding on to my coat. Just going to the commissary for food was a serious undertaking.

As the weeks dragged by, it got colder and lonelier; no word about when Ted would be returning. And then, the much-anticipated box from home arrived! My mother, as usual, came through with "home" in a box, a BIG box, a Dole banana box. It probably measured three feet by one and a half feet by at least a foot deep! A big box, loaded with presents and goodies for us all. With tears coursing down my cheeks, I took each festively wrapped item and laid it under the tree. Where did the tree come from? I have no memory of that at all. One of my friends must have brought it to me. We did try to take care of each other.

In the dental group there were two commanding officers, a Colonel and a major (who had been in the Bataan Death March) and eleven dentists in the unit, all young recent graduates from dental college, all married, all far from home, some with a child or two. By necessity we helped each other, shared babysitting, and even child care when we traveled, nursed one another as needed and in general were best friends.

Hallelujah for friends!

The Big Day approached, and still no Ted, no Daddy to play with or share the fun of decorating the tree. We were invited to join others for Christmas dinner, probably dear friends Frances and Ed Heyne, but I can't really say I remember. It was a very stressful and exhausting few weeks.

Two nights before Christmas I had finally gotten the last little girl to bed and asleep, the tree was lit with a bright glow of multi-colored lights and I was feeling very sorry for myself, and really, deservedly so. *Nowadays*, I would pour a glass of wine, put on some happy Christmas music and take a big deep breath, relax, and perhaps find a bit of peace in just being. But *then* there was no wine, no music, no peace. I had only tears to salve my aching heart and exhausted body.

Being the resourceful person I've become, however just a fledgling at that time, I did the only reasonable and sensible thing possible. I opened every gift, carefully examined it, felt the texture of fabric, the scents of pine and cinnamon, the buttons on little girls' dresses, the silky smoothness of a blouse and the rich colors of Christmas wrapping paper.

Each and every item was held dear to my heart. Little did my mother know how her carefully chosen and wrapped gifts would lift my spirit out of the doldrums. The box had taken a month to arrive from her home in Oakland, California, to my apartment in Mannheim, The Federal Republic of Germany, thousands of miles away. Many years later I sent a similar box to Karen and Kristen when they lived in Hawaii, with pine tree boughs to bring them the fragrance of a Christmas tree.

I rewrapped each and every one of the gifts and goodies to be opened and savored when Ted returned, still TBD (to be determined). Since the girls had no sense of time or dates, I let Christmas slip by and even took the three of them to the Sunday "family night" at the Officer's Club for dinner.

It turned out that was ill advised. Kristen often had a sensitive digestive system to say the least. When she was born, she had to undergo major surgery to remove a large tumor on her neck and then a second surgery to remove "fingers" or roots of the tumor behind her esophagus. The doctors surmised that the long-term effects of the anesthesia created her sensitivity to some foods. We later found she was lactose intolerant; that explained a lot...later, but not at the time.

We had just finished dinner when Kristen called to me with a stricken look on her face and promptly threw up on the table. Fortunately, it was covered with a table cloth which I quickly folded up over everything and just sat there, mortified. A woman with a small child on her arm came over to me and in a quiet voice reassured me we were all parents and these things happen.

Upon saying this her small daughter let loose and a drizzle of urine ran down the woman's arm and onto her dress. We both just broke up laughing and the moment of embarrassment was over! But not the mess of course. I was inclined to try to do something, anything to clean it up or make it go away. A gracious waitress saved me from further anguish by coming by, bussing the dishes, and whisking away the offending tablecloth.

By then I had determined my best and only option was to just leave. Which I did, not so promptly as I would have wished, as I still had to bundle up three kids in snow worthy clothing, trundle them out to our freezing cold car and drive the five or so minutes back to the apartment.

Where. Was. My. Husband?

I needed him to help me, I was coping but it was becoming more difficult by the day. Reflecting back on that time I guess it was more the emotional support I needed. I was physically able to manage, but just barely. Ted always bathed the two older girls, "painted" bubble mustaches on their cherubic faces, and dried and powdered them. Kristen was toilet trained for daytime but still required a night diaper; that was my job, then Ted got them into their footed jammies and ready for the nighttime reading ritual.

But with him gone, once their bath and bedtime routines were all accomplished, I had but a few hours to myself to catch my breath, read and write letters from and to home, plus manage a dozen other mundane tasks.

I needed a real break. It finally came right after the New Year 1960. I got word that Ted's ship – wait - SHIP?? had docked at Bremerhaven and he would be home in a day, arriving by train.

He had left New York or thereabouts a bit less than two weeks previously and spent the time traversing the Atlantic in the middle of winter, not a pleasant experience on a troop ship in high seas.

He found himself as the ranking officer on the ship and thus was required to do inspections and whatever else was the responsibility of the Officer of the Day. He had no clue! He was a dentist, well suited for an organized and sanitary operatory.

This was a noisy, rather unsanitary group of very seasick soldiers who, I'm sure, wondered what the heck they were doing over Christmas on this miserable voyage. But fortunately, there are those of a certain rank and military experience who truly run the ship; one Chief Petty Officer in particular understood his dilemma and would say things like, "Sir, usually we ....; or, "it is time to..." in the morning or afternoon or whenever, or "Sir, I've prepared these .... for your signature", saving Ted face and dignity over and over.

It was a cold blustery day when he was picked up at the Mannheim train station and delivered into our grateful arms. The following day, after a hearty breakfast, we opened our Christmas gifts.

Oh, what lovely surprises for everyone as we unwrapped the precious reminders of family. There were gifts from home, plus a few extras Ted had bought while he was there, and those I had for him and the girls.

How could I possibly forget any hour of that month? It truly was the most memorable Christmas I've ever experienced. There have been dozens of Christmas holiday gatherings in the interim. Sadly, we lost our beloved Kristen in a car crash in 1997, just shortly before Christmas. Karen and Leslie are now retired and enjoying grandchildren, and I've been the proud matriarch of our family all these years.

Ms. Embree has enjoyed the many benefits of traveling the world over, having been on six of the seven continents. Her interest in seeing the world is summed up by these favorite quotes about travel: "I am not the same having seen the moon shine on the other side of the world" (Anonymous); as well as "Travel makes one modest, you see what a tiny place you occupy in the world" (Gustave Flaubert).

Judith lives in Rancho Murieta with her two cats, Leo and The Princess. She is a graduate of the University of San Francisco, also a retiree from the California Youth Authority. Ms. Embree enjoys reading, quilting and cooking but primarily spending time with her family and friends.

This is her first published work.

WHITE CHRISTMAS MORN'

SANDRA D. SIMMER

His ear-piercing howls often
carried by a frantic gale alert
all in his path to seek shelter.

Other times he is silent, secretive,
his quiet travels go unheard.

The solitary visitor arrives on a breeze
and drags his long white beard of
frozen crystals across the night sky.

He shakes his head to free a trillion
tiny particles of ice to float to earth
light as feathers released
from pillows of clouds overhead.

The cascade of whiteness covers rooftops.
Houses disappear under deep piles of cold,
while residents dream undisturbed.

Tree branches are cloaked by
a heavy wet blanket of frost.

The shape of the familiar is transformed
Into the unrecognizable.

That which is unclean or ugly becomes
something serene and beautiful.

The unsuspecting sleepers wake
to gaze upon a frozen fairyland and
marvel at the magic created by
Winter's newly fallen snow.

CINNAMON COFFEE

JACKIE ALCALDE MARR

January 20, 2020
Atlanta, Georgia

S ue took a sip, closed her eyes, and said, "Oh my gosh, you make the best coffee."

"I sprinkle just a little cinnamon on the grounds. My grandma said that her grandma learned that on the plantation, and the secret has been passed down through the generations." Kristy winked at Sue while she buttered her bagel.

"I like what you've done there." Sue nodded to the wall opposite them in the kitchen. Three large, silver frames hung side by side. On the left was a sepia photograph of a cream-skinned woman with her grey hair in a tight bun, the collar of her crisp blouse high against her neck. On the right was the iconic Dr. Martin Luther King, Jr., with his suit, narrow tie, and dark, determined eyes. Between the two was a letter on yellowed parchment, its precise cursive was faint but still readable behind the glass. Above the arrangement was a wooden sign with the words "Always Dream!" scrolled upon it.

Kristy smiled and sighed. "He's amazing, of course. But, you know, *she's* my hero. I still can't believe all that happened in her lifetime. The years leading up to the civil war must have been incredibly tough."

"Especially for women," Sue chimed in.

Kristy felt her heart pound faster. It always did when she thought of Anabel. "I'm grateful that her story has been passed down through my family. Gosh, four generations now. And, if you hadn't brought those letters from your great, great grandmother, we would have never known some of the details."

"I'm just glad Elizabeth saved those letters, and that the researcher I hired actually found you!" Sue said, cradling the coffee mug in her hand. "Please, tell me the story again."

"I guess we've got some time before we need to leave," Kristy said. She poured more coffee for the two of them and let the story unfold.

~ * ~ * ~ * ~ *

January 16, 1860
Nelson Plantation, Atlanta Georgia

Anabel sat at the desk, instinctively glancing over her shoulder to be sure she was alone in the great room. Harley, the foreman, was already in the fields. Trina had cleared away breakfast and was no doubt scrubbing the floors in the kitchen. Anabel relaxed just a bit and continued writing her letter.

"I tell you, dear Elizabeth, that I've never seen such brutality inflicted on another human being in all my life! I can imagine the need to keep a strict operation on this huge house and plantation. It must be very difficult. But I can't help but shudder at the tactics. Well, it's certainly not my place to offer any thoughts on the matter. And I hope to be home soon.

Since Uncle Charles passed last year, Aunt Mary has had such a tough go of it. And now the poor thing can barely keep broth in her belly. I thought I was summoned here to nurse her back to health, but I dare say I'm too late. The doctors here must not be as proficient as ours in Boston, and..."

"She's askin' for you, Miss Anabel." Trina stood in the doorway, wiping her hands on her apron.

"Thank you, Trina." Anabel stood up, folded the letter neatly, and put it into her skirt pocket as she began up the sweeping staircase.

In the bedroom, she pulled the chair up close to the bed. She watched Trina arrange the quilts and gently lift her aunt to place two more pillows behind her head and shoulders. "Are you comfortable, ma'am? Can I get you anythin' else?" Anabel noticed Trina's soft voice, and the way she smoothed Aunt Mary's hair back from her forehead. How old was she? Eighteen? Twenty? Although she was just a housemaid, a slave born into this plantation, she looked at Mary, her...owner...with true affection.

"No, Trina. I'm fine. Thank you so much." Aunt Mary smiled at the girl.

"Then I'll be in the kitchen, snappin' peas. You be sure to ring the bell if you be needin' anythin' at all." Trina gave a nod to Anabel as she left the room.

"How are you feeling, Auntie?" Anabel took her aunt's hand, cold and fragile.

"I'm okay, child," Aunt Mary replied, then coughed violently, dislodging the carefully placed pillow behind her head.

Anabel returned the pillow to its place, trying to be as gentle as Trina had been. She handed her aunt a glass of water that Trina had thoughtfully left on the nightstand, just within her aunt's reach.

Aunt Mary took a sip and her shaking hand let a few drops splash on the nightstand when she put it down. Then she grasped Anabel's hand and looked her in the eyes. Anabel was shocked at how strong those cold hands were.

"Listen to me, child. I'm afraid I will not last many more days on this earth, and..."

"Don't say that Auntie," Anabel interrupted. She tried to sound sincere, but she knew her aunt was probably right.

"Shush now, Ana. It's okay. I'll soon be with your Uncle Charles, and we will both be happy again." She paused, cleared her throat, and then continued. "I'm worried about the plantation. Since we've not been blessed with children, they will try to turn the property over to Harley. He's been the foreman here for more than eighteen years, and it will seem logical to everyone. But it's not logical to me!" She coughed then grimaced, as though the thought of this stirred up all the toxins in her body.

"That's why I'm leaving the plantation to you, my child."

The grip on her hand was strong and steady as though Aunt Mary was not going to let her shy from this gift. Gift? Or burden? Anabel was dumbfounded.

"But Auntie, I don't know anything about running a plantation. I would simply defer to Harley anyway for all the decisions and the managing of the..." She paused as the image of yesterday's incident flashed before her.

A young slave boy had placed the chopped wood in the wrong place. From his perch on his chestnut horse, Harley had kicked the boy. The boy fell to the ground, but scrambled back up again, keeping his eyes to the dirt, and crying "I'm sorry! I'll get it right nex' time." Blood dribbled from his split lip, slid down his chin, and created a little burst of dust as it hit the ground. Anabel had run out the door to reprimand Harley, but she stopped at the edge of the porch, trying not to cry. This wasn't her home, and Harley would have just laughed at her.

She shook the image from her mind and continued, "...the managing of the workers. Surely, he knows the best way to run things. I feel I'd only be in the way."

"Anabel." Her aunt shook her hand with fervor. "Charles and I adored each other, but there was one thing we differed on greatly – the way to manage this plantation. We have always treated our slaves well. But once Charles passed, and the tensions between the South and the North grew, Harley took it upon himself to do things his own way. I tried to set him straight, but I fell ill before I could muster enough strength. It will surely be my one regret. Come now, I know you see that his tactics are a little extreme."

A little? Anabel was relieved to know that her aunt saw the brutality, but still dismayed that her response was so subdued. Still, what could her aunt have done? And what could she possibly do to shift Harley's tactics? For all she knew, he was right, and this was the only way to keep such an operation successful.

"But, Auntie, I'm not sure I can do anything to..."

"Shush, child. I'm tired. I must sleep now. The lawyers and the judge will be here in the morning." Aunt Mary looked fierce for a moment, her eyes locking on Anabel's. "But hear me, Ana – you have more strength than you know. And you must use it…"

The grip on Anabel's hand went slack. Aunt Mary's voice trailed off, and she drifted to sleep.

~ ~ ~ ~

January 17, 1860

Aunt Mary put the pen down and sighed with exhaustion. "There now. You've all witnessed that my niece, Anabel, is now the sole proprietor of this plantation, and she has every right to manage it as she pleases."

The men in the room nodded in Anabel's direction. She held her head high because she knew Aunt Mary would want that, but inside she felt like a wilted leaf. Somewhat against her will, her life had suddenly changed. It was unsettling to not have agency over your own life. And she thought of Trina and the boy from the other day and all the other slaves. What agency had they ever had?

Anabel led the men to the front door, the lawyers tipped their hats and trotted down the stairs. Judge Henshaw stood on the porch and spoke with a sympathetic voice, "I know this is new to you, Miss Anabel. But we are all very fond of your aunt, and we are here to help you in any way that…"

Just then a crash came from the kitchen, and Trina cried out, "Please Massa Harley!"

"Excuse me," Anabel turned from the doorway and ran into the kitchen.

A chair laid toppled on the floor, and Harley stood with his back to the doorway, towering over Trina, his left hand on her wrist as she flailed. Anabel grabbed a cast iron skillet from the shelf and slammed it down on the table. Harley turned, still clutching Trina's wrist with his fat fingers. Trina's blouse had been torn; her bare shoulder revealed. Harley began to laugh.

"Mr. Harley!" Anabel tried to maintain a steady voice, but it was much higher pitched and louder than she'd intended. "You will leave this property at once! You are no longer employed here."

Harley let go of Trina and took two slow steps toward Anabel. He sneered, "Who do you think you are, missy?"

Anabel picked up the cast iron pan and held it beside her shoulder, ready to swing if necessary.

"She's the owner and manager of this plantation, Harley." Judge Henshaw's voice came from behind her. "I think you'd best do as she says. You no longer have a place here." He walked forward, taking the pan from Anabel's shaking hand, and placing it gently on the table.

Harley stood dumbfounded. Trina gathered her torn blouse and bowed her head.

"Get your things and go, Mr. Harley. I want you out by supper time." Anabel squared her shoulders and willed her lips not to quiver. She felt dizzy and put her hand on the table to steady herself.

Harley stood for a moment as though trying to decide how to protest. Then he simply huffed and stormed out the back door, banging it against the exterior wall.

"Go get yourself together, Trina." Anabel said softly as she saw the tear slip down Trina's cheek. Judge Henshaw stepped aside so that Trina could slip by them, her eyes never leaving the floor.

Anabel and Judge Henshaw stood silent for a long moment. Then he picked up the chair from the floor, placed it gingerly at the table, and held Anabel's hand to seat her. She collected her wits, clasped her hands tightly and laid them on the table. Then she gave him a cordial smile.

"I'll send an officer to stand post on your porch tonight. Don't you worry about Harley. We'll make sure he moves on." He covered her clasped hands with his own large palm. It was warm and heavy, and Anabel felt his strength. He was kind – a good man. They looked at each other without speaking. Their eyes conveyed the agreement that a sentry would be a good idea.

~ ~ ~ ~

The fire snapped and sputtered as the logs shifted.

Anabel sat in one of the wing chairs beside the hearth and read the words she'd written that afternoon.

"What am I to do, Elizabeth? I am most certainly a fish out of water. This plantation is small compared to its neighbors, but it still requires a business mind. I'm afraid I have not the intelligence nor the courage, if I'm truthful, to maintain its productivity."

"Excuse me, Miss Anabel. Jus' wanted you to know that she's sleepin' now. Her breathin' is still labored, but she has found some rest." Trina carried a tray with a coffee pot, cup, and saucer and placed it on the small table beside Anabel's chair. She gave a slight curtsy and turned to leave.

"Trina." Anabel folded her letter and slipped it into her skirt pocket. "Your coffee smells so good. Is that cinnamon?"

"Yes, ma'am. My mamma taught me to put a little pinch on the grounds."

"How clever!" Anabel continued, "Trina, would you please get another cup from the kitchen and join me?"

Trina's eyes flickered with confusion. Then she smiled, "I'll be right back, Miss Anabel."

Anabel picked up the small table with its tray and placed it in front of the fireplace so it could be reached from both wing chairs. Trina returned with another cup and saucer, and her mouth fell open to see the placement of the tray.

"Please," Anabel gestured to the other chair.

Trina moved cautiously. She put her cup and saucer on the tray, then poured the hot coffee into each cup. She took the lid off the sugar bowl, raising her eyebrows to Anabel in question. Anabel shook her head and waved her hand. Trina looked into the sugar bowl and hesitated. She licked her lips, then put the lid back in place.

Anabel watched as Trina sat erect on the edge of the other chair. A moment later Trina spoke. "I thank you, Miss Anabel, for what you did this mornin'."

Anabel sipped the hot coffee, then put her cup and saucer on the tray. She stared into the fire. Then, she turned to Trina. She pursed her lips and shook her head slowly. "I'm so sorry," she said, looking into Trina's eyes. They glistened with tears.

Trina took a sip of her coffee as though looking for something to do to ease the moment.

After another long pause, Anabel said, "May I confess something, Trina?"

"Of course, ma'am." Trina said softly.

"I'm scared." Anabel took another sip of coffee. "I don't know a thing about running a plantation. I'm afraid I won't be able to maintain its prosperity."

Trina stared into the fire, then put her cup down on the tray. "Miss Anabel." She paused and looked directly into Anabel's eyes. My, the girl's stare was captivating.

Trina swallowed before saying, "I ain' never seen a woman as brave as you."

Anabel let the words sink in, wanting to believe they were true.

Trina bowed her head, but looked up sheepishly, "For a moment I thought you was gonna kill Massa Harley."

Then they both smiled devilishly.

"Truthfully, I don't know what I would have done if the judge hadn't come in," said Anabel, looking back to the fire.

"Listen to me, Miss Anabel." Trina leaned forward. "The runnin' of the plantation ain' no big thing. All of us been doin' that for years. But since Massa Charles passed, and Miss Mary took ill, it's been hard to feel this a home." Trina paused and tipped her cup back to get the last drop. "You have no idea the fresh air you brought to this place. I'm not real strong, but I'll help you howeva I can."

Anabel reached across the table and refilled Trina's cup. Anabel saw Trina straighten uncomfortably at the gesture. "Trina, my aunt told me this, and now I tell you – you are much stronger than you think."

She reached across the tray and lifted the lid of the sugar bowl. "Please," she gestured an invitation to Trina.

~ ~ ~ ~

"Last night I had a fitful sleep, tossing and turning. I dreamt a man was standing on a platform, and he looked

onto a river of sorts, and he spoke to a vast crowd of people. He said that he had a dream. And the people cheered. And, Elizabeth, they were negroes and white people, both. But the more shocking thing was that the man was a negro! Oh, my strange head. But I woke up energized.

There is so much to learn here, Elizabeth, and yet I feel strangely calm. These people, they are just like us, really. And we will make this work – together.

After a week of writing to you, I must get this letter in the post. I hope you are well and happy.

Your dear friend,
Anabel"

~ ~ ~ ~

January 20, 2020
Atlanta, Georgia

Sue shook her head, "What a premonition she had! It's amazing that she and the judge married and eventually gave the plantation to Trina! I didn't know slaves could inherit property back then."

"After the war, it was possible for freed slaves to have property of their own. And since Anabel and the judge never had children of their own, I suppose it made sense. Still, I'm sure it was a brave move. My great, great grandmother must have been so surprised."

Sue put her cup in the sink and said, "Dr. King would have loved Trina and Anabel. C'mon," she picked up her poster that read The Dream Lives On! "Let's go, the march is about to start."

Kristy grabbed her keys from the table by the front door. The table was covered with photographs of Kristy's family – all ebony-skinned. Stoic women with small children and elderly couples smiling. And one very special photo, an old one, of Trina and Anabel on the porch with their coffee cups in hand.

Jackie loves wine, nurturing old friendships, all things Spain, and the lessons found in history. She is a lifelong learner and loves to pack her bag for adventure.

After a long corporate career as an organization development consultant, Jackie created Evolutions Consulting Group. As an independent consultant, trainer, and certified leadership/life coach, she helps individuals and groups achieve their goals while accentuating their core passions. She works with private, public, and non-profit organizations, as well as individuals who are creating fulfilling lives.

Jackie has been published in the Sacramento Business magazine and the Organization Development Journal. She also co-authored *Social Media At Work: How Networking Tools Propel Organizational Performance* (Jossey-Bass).

She's currently writing the story of her family's immigration from Spain to Hawaii and then California and a memoir for her young granddaughter. She lives in Folsom with her husband Jeff and their mischievous mutt, Quincy Noodlebutt.

GRANDMA HANNAH'S THANKSGIVING VISIT

CHARLENE JOHNSON

"Dinner was great," Dex Brooks said as he helped his wife, Felicity, clear the dinner dishes.

"Thanks, honey. I've been trying out some new recipes."

"That caramel apple pie was to die for."

"Wait until tomorrow," Felicity said. "I have another new dessert planned."

He set the dishes in the sink and patted his stomach. "I must start cutting logs for the winter. It's the only way I can work off those delicious desserts."

"Having fresh fruit from our garden, and eggs from our chickens makes all the difference. It inspires me."

"My mom always had a garden when I was growing up. We never bought fruit or vegetables at the grocery store. I'm glad we're able to freeze a fair amount of our fruit and vegetables. It reminds me of home."

Felicity smirked. "My mom didn't have a green thumb. She killed every house plant we ever had."

"Then why are you so good at it?"

"My grandma. The green thumb skipped a generation. I used to garden with her whenever I went to visit."

"I love your Grandma Hannah. She's quite the character."

Felicity laughed. "Grandma is the adventurous one in the family, and it drives my mom crazy. About five years ago, Grandma decided to go on a safari in Africa with a tour group. She told me it was something she's wanted to do ever since she watched the movie, *The African Queen*."

"Is that with Humphrey Bogart and Katharine

Hepburn?"

Felicity nodded. "That's the one. I watched it with her as a kid. It is a great movie."

"Did your parents go with her?" Dex asked.

"No. Grandma insisted she go alone. She's always loved meeting new people, and she said my mom would cramp her style."

"Good for her."

"Mom was a nervous wreck and insisted Grandma call her every day, but it was impossible. There were some places on the tour where the phone reception was nonexistent. Grandma called as much as she could, but Mom wasn't too happy about it. My grandpa would have gone with her had he lived, but he died ten years ago. I think that's the reason she went. They were planning to go on a safari before Grandpa passed. She was fulfilling one thing on their bucket list."

Dex grinned. "It makes me admire your grandma even more. You should ask her to come for a visit. We haven't seen her since last Thanksgiving at your folks' house."

Felicity nodded. "I know. I'd like to see her before the winter comes. I miss her."

"Why not call her and invite her for Thanksgiving with us? My parents are coming. My brothers are spending the holiday weekend hiking in British Columbia with some of their buddies."

"Dex, that's a great idea. Mom and Dad are going on a cruise this year, and Bobby's girlfriend invited him to her parents' house. It will be his first time meeting her family."

"Is it getting serious between them?"

"Bobby told me it was."

"Then why isn't Grandma Hannah going with your parents?" Dex asked.

"My mom would drive her crazy fussing over her. The cruise ship isn't big enough for my grandma to get away from her."

Dex laughed out loud. "All the more reason to invite Grandma here."

*   *   *

Felicity called her grandmother the next day, and left a message because there was no answer.

Her grandma returned the call later in the evening.

"Hello, Felicity."

"Hi, Grandma. You got my message."

"I did."

"Are you going to come here for Thanksgiving?"

"I'd love to, sweetie. I had no plans. Your mom tried to talk me into going with her and Carl on their cruise. No way I was doing that. Don't get me wrong, I love my daughter and my son-in-law, but they treat me like a decrepit little old lady who can't take care of herself."

"That's definitely not you."

Grandma Hannah laughed. "I wish I could convince Mary of that."

"I think Mom is afraid you're doing too much."

"She's going to have to get over it. I don't plan to slow down until I'm dead. I want to enjoy my life as long as I can."

"I don't blame you. Just let me know when your flight gets in so we can pick you up."

"I'll make reservations for early Monday morning so I can help you get a head start on Thanksgiving dinner."

"Grandma, I want you to relax while you're here. I don't expect you to cook."

"Felicity, I want to be helpful. Besides, it's more time I get to spend with you."

"You know I'll love that. I remember the weekends I spent with you. Those were the happiest times of my life."

"I miss those weekends too," her grandmother agreed.

"I almost forgot to mention Dex's parents are coming for Thanksgiving too."

"How wonderful! I look forward to seeing them again."

"Can't wait to see you, Grandma."

"Me either."

"Love you."

"Love you too, Felicity."

*   *   *

Felicity was collecting eggs in the chicken coop when she felt an odd flutter. Setting down the basket, she placed her hands over her lower abdomen. When it happened again, she knew what she'd suspected for over a month was true.

"I'm pregnant!" Felicity exclaimed with elation and wonder.

Her excitement quickly turned to apprehension. Her pregnancy was not going to be a normal one. She and Dex were shapeshifters, and she had no idea what to expect.

Picking up the basket of eggs, she left the chicken coop and walked through the ivy-covered arbor to the secret garden. It was the sanctuary Dex created for her as a birthday surprise last year. She'd spent many sunny days reading there. It was also the place she went when she needed to think.

Placing the wicker basket beside her, Felicity sat down on the wooden bench Dex had fashioned out of a fallen tree from their forest. Her heart was beating rapidly in her chest, and she tried to focus on the Italian-inspired water fountain surrounded by wild lavender roses. The sound of the water trickling down the three-tiered perfection was soothing. Breathing in deeply, she wished for calm.

She wanted to call her mother, but her parents were already on the cruise ship. Not that it mattered. How could she talk to her about her pregnancy? Her mother couldn't answer the unusual barrage of questions Felicity had. How long would her pregnancy last? Would she go to full term as other humans, or would it be shorter? Would the baby shift immediately after birth? How many babies would she have? Her mind was spinning with questions.

Dex's parents would be there Wednesday. Emma Brooks was the only female shapeshifter Felicity knew. She would have to wait until Emma arrived. It was something Felicity wanted to discuss with her mother-in-law face to face before she told Dex. They'd been married for a little over three years and they looked forward to having a baby.

But it hadn't happened. Until now.

Grandma Hannah would be there before Dex's parents, but Felicity's pregnancy was the one thing she couldn't talk to Grandma about. The thought made Felicity a little sad.

"Nothing I can do about it now," Felicity whispered in a low voice, placing a hand over her abdomen again. "You'll have to be my little secret for two more days."

"What secret is that?" Dex asked when he appeared in the garden.

Felicity's head snapped up in surprise. "Dex, you scared me."

"You must have been deep in thought," he teased, sitting next to her.

She smiled. "I was thinking about what desserts I am going to make for Thanksgiving. Since Grandma is going to be here, I thought she and I could bake her delicious peach cobbler. We used to pick peaches from the tree in her back yard and make cobbler from scratch. It was always my favorite dessert and I think you'll love it. I have some sliced peaches in the freezer. They should be perfect for Grandma's cobbler."

"That was your secret?"

Felicity nodded. "Yes," she lied. "I was talking to myself. I wanted it to be a surprise."

Dex chuckled. "I didn't hear you mention peach cobbler but I'm looking forward to it."

"Then you must have only heard the end of it. Come," she said as she stood quickly, picking up the wicker basket. "I need to finish collecting eggs if you want breakfast this morning."

* * *

"Grandma, it's so good to have you here," Felicity declared as the three of them sat down for a late afternoon lunch.

"We missed you," Dex added. "We're so happy you agreed to come to our farm for Thanksgiving. Felicity has been anxious for you to see it." He reached across the table to grip his wife's hand. "She's quite the farmer."

Grandma Hannah grinned. "My Felicity has always loved the outdoors. We spent a lot of time in my garden. She was ever the avid student."

"I loved those weekends, Grandma."

"When Felicity grew up and went to college all the way across the country in California, I really missed her."

Felicity's face grew serious. "It was something I had to do."

"I know you must have had your reasons, but it didn't stop me from missing you."

"If Felicity hadn't moved to San Francisco, I would never have met her," Dex added.

"That's true," Grandma Hannah agreed. "I've always wanted her to be happy."

"I am happy," Felicity replied, smiling at Dex. "Happier than I thought was possible."

"I'm so glad to hear it." She winked at Dex. "My grandson-in-law is quite the catch."

"Grandma," Felicity began as they finished lunch, "why don't you go rest for a little while before I give you a tour of the farm? You must be tired from your flight."

"I'm not tired, sweetie. I'd love to see it."

Dex stood up. "Why don't you two go? I'll clear the table?"

Felicity frowned, studying her grandmother. "Are you sure?"

"Felicity," Grandma Hannah said in a teasing voice. "You're starting to sound like your mother."

"Sorry," Felicity said apologetically. "I didn't mean to."

Grandma Hannah stood up and reached for Felicity's hand. "I'll forgive you this one time," she replied with amusement.

"I promise not to do it again," her granddaughter replied mischievously. "I hate it when I hear my mother's words coming out of my mouth. I love her dearly but she's a worry wart."

"I love your mother, too. Don't worry, you are more like me and that's a good thing."

* * *

"I can see why you and Dex love it here so much," Grandma Hannah said as she and Felicity passed the chicken coop and the gated area where Daisy, the cow, was grazing.

"Dex's father and his brothers helped him build the coop and fenced in the areas for our other animals. They also helped him build the garden's planter boxes and the surrounding fence to keep the local white-tailed deer out."

"Felicity, I don't want to change the subject, but I could tell something was bothering you during lunch," Grandma Hannah said abruptly.

Felicity stopped and stared at her grandma, shocked by her keen perception. All through lunch, she wanted to come clean and tell Grandma she was a shapeshifter, and share her fears regarding her pregnancy, but how could she? Grandma Hannah would never understand.

"There's nothing wrong, Grandma. I'm a little tired from getting things ready for the holiday."

"When did you find out you are pregnant?"

Felicity's hands instinctively went to her abdomen as she gaped at Grandma.

"How did you know?"

"You and I have very much in common," Grandma Hannah remarked.

"Of course, we do, Felicity laughed nervously. "We're related."

"Take me to this secret garden of yours so we can sit and talk. I have much to tell you."

When they were seated on the bench, Grandma Hannah took Felicity's hand. "There's something I've kept secret from everyone for many years."

"Even from Mom?"

"Yes, it's something your mother would never understand."

"You're scaring me, Grandma," Felicity exclaimed.

Grandma Hannah patted her hand. "It's nothing you

should be worried about. You are the one person who could identify with my secret."

Felicity frowned. "I don't understand."

"You do. I'm a shapeshifter like you."

Felicity nearly fell off the bench in shock. Grandma Hannah was a shapeshifter, just like her!

"Is Mom one too?"

"No. It sometimes skips generations. Your great, great Grandma Muriel was a shapeshifter, as was her grandmother before her. It's a family legacy that shouldn't be discussed with humans. They would never understand."

"Was Grandpa Henry a shapeshifter?"

Grandma Hannah smiled. "No, he was a human. Our relationship should never have happened, but love isn't always predictable. It doesn't fit in a perfect box."

"Did Grandpa know?"

"Yes, he did. He was the only one I told."

"I never asked you before, but how did you and Grandpa meet?"

"We met at the drive-in. I was with my boyfriend, Dale Evans, at the time."

"You dated human men?"

"Yes. Back then, it was expected for girls to date, get married and have babies. I played my role, but I never had any intentions to marry unless I found someone who was like me."

"That's something I definitely understand," Felicity commented. "Until Dex, marriage was never a possibility for me either."

"Sweetie, you are fortunate."

"Yes. I am

"I know the official story about how you and Dex met. Is there more to the story?"

Felicity smiled. "Yes. I was in the forest above San Francisco in the form of a great horned owl when I first saw Dex. I saw him shift into a red fox, and I went back to the forest often to see him. He was so handsome. I didn't realize it, but he came back there to watch me too. He told me he didn't know I was a shapeshifter at the time, but he should have. When a hunter shot me, I fell from my perch, Dex shifted and took me to a veterinarian to treat my wound."

"Was it serious?"

"No, the hunter shot my left wing, and I couldn't fly."

"You didn't shift back to human?" Grandma Hannah asked.

"No. That didn't happen until weeks later. Dex took me to his home and nursed me until I was healed. One day, he told me it was time to take me back to the forest. The realization I'd probably never see him again caused me to shift back to human. We've been together ever since."

"Your injury may have prevented you from shifting sooner," her grandmother added.

"Grandma, it was so unexpected to find out Dex and his family were shapeshifters and had been for generations. Especially after I thought I was the only one in our family. I didn't feel alone anymore."

"I knew they were like us the first time I met them at the wedding, and that you were going to be okay."

Felicity smiled. "You sensed them just as Dex and his family can."

"Yes. It was something my grandmother taught me."

"I'm learning to be more perceptive. Being with Dex has helped me."

"That's wonderful."

"Please, Grandma, continue your story about meeting Grandpa."

Grandma Hannah smiled as her eyes grew animated. "I went to the concession stand to get popcorn and a strawberry milkshake when I saw him. He was the most handsome guy I'd ever seen, with his chestnut hair and hazel eyes. He was with a bunch of his friends. They were laughing and playing around when our eyes met. He grinned, and I nearly lost my breath. Next thing I knew, he approached me. He introduced himself and asked if I was at the drive-in alone. I told him I was with my boyfriend. The cashier came back to the counter with my popcorn and milkshake. Afraid Dale would come looking for me, I grabbed my snacks and left the concession stand. I looked back to where your grandpa was standing, and he was still looking at me. It made me blush."

"What happened after that?" Felicity asked. "When did you see him again?"

"Believe it or not, at the local diner three weeks later. After seeing him at the drive-in, I couldn't stop thinking about him. I broke up with my boyfriend, hoping I would see Henry again. I almost gave up hope until he entered the diner alone. He was picking up an order. Afraid he wouldn't see me, I went up to the counter. The smile on his face when he saw me lit up my world. He asked me out and eventually we got married and were together until the day he died."

Grandma, how long were you together before you told him you were a shapeshifter?"

"The day he asked me to marry him. I couldn't say yes until he knew the truth."

"How did he react?"

"Henry thought I was joking at first, so I had to show him. We drove to the park and found a small, secluded clearing surrounded by tall trees. I shifted into a border collie. I used that form often. It was nonthreatening and made it easy for me to blend into the neighborhood where we lived. Henry was shocked and a little frightened, but he didn't run away.

Understandably, he said he needed time to think, so we ended our date. I didn't see him for weeks. I was beginning to think it was over between us, and it broke my heart. But he showed up at my parents' house and asked to talk to me. We went for a walk in the park. He asked me a lot of questions and I answered them as best as I could. He told me he loved me and didn't care what I was. He got on one knee right there in the park and again asked me to marry him. I cheerfully said yes. We had such a happy life together."

"When you got pregnant with Mom, were you worried?" Felicity asked.

"Not really," Grandma Hannah replied. "My grandmother told me what to expect. She also married a human man. She said our children could either be human or shapeshifters. Your mom turned out to be human. You won't have to worry about that. Your baby will be a shapeshifter since you both are."

"I'm worried about the pregnancy. I don't know what to expect," Felicity exclaimed anxiously.

"No need to worry. It will be fine. You will have a shorter pregnancy than a human woman. Full term for us is six months."

"What about Mom? Won't she be suspicious?"

Grandma Hannah shrugged. "She'll just think your baby is premature."

"Is it possible I could have twins like Dex's mother did?"

Her grandmother nodded. "It's very possible. Would that bother you?"

"No, Grandma. I was so apprehensive because I didn't think I had anyone but Dex's mom to talk to about it. I spent so much time over the years keeping my secret from Mom, Dad, and Bobby."

"I'm so sorry, Felicity, I blame myself for not being more forthcoming with you. I should have talked to you about what you were, but you wouldn't have understood it until you shifted for the first time. I was also afraid you would tell your parents, and that would have been disastrous. How would I have explained it to Mary? She would never have understood. Perhaps, it never should have been kept a secret, but it wasn't as simple as telling your family members they might be susceptible to kidney stones. When you moved away, I assumed you figured it out. Then you married Dex, and I stopped worrying. You had him and his family to lean on. Please don't be angry with me for not telling you. I love you so much."

Felicity hugged her. "I'm not angry, Grandma. I love you too. Perhaps the secret we shared is why we've always been so close."

"I promise you, Felicity, I'll be here when you give birth. If you want, I'll come the month before and stay for a little while after your baby is born to help out."

Felicity beamed. "I'd love that!"

"Besides, someone has to save you from your mother's

constant fussing."

She laughed. "So true. I'll definitely need someone to run interference."

"There's enough to do on your farm to keep her occupied and she loves to sew. I'll have her making baby clothes."

"Thank you, Grandma. What would I do without you?"

"I'm always here for you." Grandma Hannah stood up. "Let's go back to the house. I think it's time you told your husband the happy news."

Charlene Johnson is a romance author recently transplanted from Sacramento, California, to Washington state. She published four books in her Paranormal Romance series - Circle of the Red Scorpion, one in her Romantic Suspense series - Sterling Wood, and a book in a multi-author series, Crimes of Passion. She also published three short stories and three poems.

Homecoming, Book 1 in her Sterling Wood series was named a Book Excellence Award finalist in the Romance category.

Books have been her passion since age nine. Being a daydreamer and an incurable romantic with a Cinderella complex, Charlene started creating her own characters and storylines because she realized she had her own stories to tell.

Her quote - *I've traveled the world, crossed galaxies, traveled through time and explored history on the pages of books.*

Besides reading and writing, Charlene also enjoys photography, travel, music, and Elvis.

Websites:
https://www.charlenejohnsonbooks.com
https://www.circleoftheredscorpion.com
https://www.sterlingwoodseries.com

Email:
circleoftheredscorpion@gmail.com

THE WAYWARD LEAF

NORMA JEAN THORNTON

The leaf was ready to get off his tree
He wanted to roam and to be set free

Mister Wind blew that leaf right down to the ground
Where it tossed and tumbled, around and around

But the Wayward Leaf had a mind of his own
And he didn't like going where he was blown

When he finally stopped, the leaf looked up
Right in the face of a Rottweiler pup!

That pup took one lick, the leaf stuck to his tongue
The pup spit it out, and away it was flung

But then the wind started blowing again
And blew that leaf to the muddy pig pen

A lady came by with her son named Buddy
She picked up the leaf before it got muddy

The leaf was unusual so she took it home
To share with more leaves in a round Styrofoam

Scary decorations joined that pretty orange leaf
And before he knew it, he was part of a wreath

There were ghosts and goblins, a spectacular sight
With the scary leaf-wreath on the door that dark night

It was Halloween the special night of fright
The wind was still blowing, but the leaf stuck tight

The leaf suddenly realized just what he had
Belonging to something wasn't so bad

It was fun watching those kids that his wreath had scared
The Wayward Leaf wasn't free, but he no longer cared

115

ANOTHER CHRISTMAS CAROL

SUSAN BETH FURST

I'm standing alone in front of the congregation of Mount Zion Evangelical Lutheran Church. I look for my dad, but everything is pitch black except for a single candle at the end of each pew. I wonder if I will remember the words as I open my mouth and sing.

"What child is this…"

Ralph and George are sitting together in the front pew. They used to sit across the aisle from one another until they tripped Pastor Fattman with a fishing line. The Pastor says we should forgive our enemies, but I guess he isn't taking any chances.

"Where ox and ass are feeding…"

My dad says it's okay to say "that word," especially in a Christmas carol on Christmas Eve. He tells me it's another word for donkey, but I ask Jesus for forgiveness, just in case.

"Nails, spear shall pierce Him through…"

Somewhere, behind me in the darkness, the choir is singing. Their voices are wobbly and out of tune. I don't like this verse. What do nails, and spears have to do with Christmas anyway?

"Joy, joy for Christ is born…"

The congregation is singing *Silent Night*. It's after midnight when we blow out our candles. Ralph and George lead the procession to the back of the church. Pastor Fattman is still on his feet. And Dad and I run to the car for the long ride home. I ask him about the nails, and he smiles as the taillights in front of us disappear in the falling snow.

Susan Beth Furst is an award-winning Japanese short-form poet and Children's Picture Book author. She has published three haiku collections: *Souvenir Shop, Road to Utopia,* and *Neon Snow.*

Her books for children include *The Amazing Glass House* and *The Hole in My Haiku.* Susan was chosen to read her haibun, *Babylon,* for the David Labkovski Project's 2021 Holocaust Remembrance Day Commemoration Program. You can view the commemoration program and journal at davidlabkovskiproject.org.

Susan lives in Fishersville, Virginia, located in the beautiful Shenandoah Valley. You can also find Susan and her books at PaperWhistlePress.com.

GOLFING IN REVERSE

DENISE LEE BRANCO

Ever had that sinking feeling something isn't quite right? You might accept and roll with the unfamiliarity at first, but when the proverbial lightbulb shines bright upon your intuition and what you knew all along, it could become the funniest one-of-a-kind adventure of your lifetime.

When my dad retired from ranching, he took up a new sport, one he had always wanted to learn—golf. He'd play weekly with friends who were at various skill levels and could teach him the game. They'd golf at out-of-town courses as a day outing, ending with conversation over a meal.

Aside from miniature golf, I had never played real golf, but had become inspired by my father's newfound love for the sport. I enjoyed watching him talk about how far he could hit the ball or how his score was improving. I'd often find him watching professional golf on TV when I'd drop by his home. I'd get a kick out of how he'd explain the pros' executed techniques to me.

I asked if we could go to our local golf course, Turkey Creek, so I could learn to play. He said the driving range would be the best place to start. I think it may have been the many years I played softball that led me to believe I was qualified to swing a golf club without much practice, because I had no desire after two times at the driving range to keep practicing. I was ready to move on and play an actual round. Since Father's Day was one week away, I knew the perfect gift—a father-daughter golfing excursion.

Dad had wanted to play golf at the Turkey Creek course but never had an opportunity. We arrived and headed to the check-in desk for our 7 a.m. tee time. We asked the reservation desk clerk for directions to the Back 9 (where management requests novices, like me, begin). The theory behind that approach was for newbies like us to get further down the course, way ahead of the advanced players so we wouldn't slow their game with our multiple attempts at moving the golf ball to the hole. Plus, beginning at the Back 9 in the early morning was part of a fun package called the *Back 9 Breakfast Deal* where breakfast was included in the greens fee.

The reservation desk clerk pointed to the right front corner of the golf shop and said, "Go that way and take a left at the turn." We thanked her and hopped in the complimentary golf cart, our golf clubs in tow, and embarked on our first father/daughter golf game.

Dad drove as we both admired the gorgeous terrain of oak trees, fountain grasses, and ponds along the path. The course had just opened and we soon discovered that being outdoors not long after dawn was the perfect time to travel to the farthest part. Dew glistened on the freshly manicured greens, a deer herd casually grazed, tree squirrels scurried, and wild turkeys foraged.

While Dad barreled down the golf cart path in our quest to reach the Back 9 by our tee time at 7 a.m. and before anyone else, I was in awe of the picturesque scenery. I took notice of the backside of wooden signs near the path. I soon found myself turning halfway around to read them. "Huh?" I thought. "That's odd." Finally, I mentioned this interesting tidbit to my dad. "Hey, Dad. It's weird how I have to turn halfway around to read those wooden signs. One said *18*. Then, we passed *17*, and I just saw *16*."

My dad's jaw dropped in his moment of realization behind the wheel. In the distance, we noticed the golf course caretaker looking at us in a perplexed way. His golden Labrador looked just as confused. Dad sped over to the caretaker and asked, "How do we get to the 10th tee quickly?!" The caretaker answered, "Follow me!" He jumped into his golf cart, and it was pedal to the metal for all! The Lab joined in the fun and ran full speed between the golf carts. That golden canine sure looked like he was smiling with glee over his unexpected early morning adventure. We wound through oaks and redwoods, went around bunkers and drove across creeks, as squirrels scurried and woodpeckers pecked, taking every shortcut imaginable before reaching the 10th tee.

Dad and I thanked our rescuers when we arrived at our destination and waved while they made a U-turn back to resume their morning work. We stepped out of the golf cart to begin our game and burst into laughter, recapping the last few exhilarating minutes. Who knew that our first golf game antics would be the actual gift rather than the fee?

After we returned the complimentary golf cart to the storage shed, our curiosity got the better of us. We decided to search for the infamous left turn. The golf path continued up a little hill from where we had originally turned so we proceeded that way. Just over the knoll, we discovered a wooden sign in the shape of an arrow pointing to the left at the fork in the road. We looked at each other, laughed some more during a no-need-for-words moment, and then headed back down the hill to the restaurant for the breakfast we more than earned.

If you're wondering whether or not we returned to that same golf course for the Back 9 Breakfast Deal on Father's Day the following year, we did. If only the reservation desk clerk at Turkey Creek hadn't omitted a wooden directional arrow in her instructions to turn left, we'd have been more proper and cultured golfers that first year. But you know what? I know firsthand that being odd and unsophisticated is way more fun!

Denise Lee Branco is an award-winning author and inspirational speaker, who continues to believe, dream, and overcome so those who meet her recognize the possibilities within them. Denise's first book, *Horse at the Corner Post: Our Divine Journey*, won a silver medal in the Living Now Book Awards.

She is a longtime member of Northern California Publishers and Authors and a current member of several other writing and publishing organizations. She has been a contributor to multiple anthologies.

Denise is currently working on her next book *The Ride to Purpose: Finding Freedom on the Trail of Life*. She lives in the foothills of Northern California and loves biking on nature trails, foods with melted cheese, and spoiling her three rescues.

Visit www.DeniseInspiresYou.com to learn more.

DANCING LEAVES

SHELLE RENAE

W as it the rustling, dancing leaves chasing one another across the lawn like curious, playful children that first drew me to the place?

I'd always been inquisitive, but tonight more so than ever before: the last night in October.

Shadows from the old, weeping willows cast an unnerving, sinister light on the lawn of the grotesque mansion, lights glittered brilliantly in most of the downstairs windows. The rusty iron gate was ajar. A frosty chill was in the air – November was right around the corner.

"What the heck?" I found myself whispering as I slowed and hovered to observe the unusual scene.

Many a night, I'd sailed past while the shiny full moon rose high in the night sky. All of these times, I've rarely given the old place a second glance.

Perhaps it was because the moon was creating an eerie glow, or perhaps it was Halloween staring me in the face

Lights had been on in the mansion previously, but never like tonight. Always one or two in the hidden corner room. One time, the light was aglow in the attic, but never the entire first floor. The brilliance caught my eyes and slowed my wings midair.

Jamming on the brakes, I circled back to see what I could see.

Cautiously I hovered over the "no trespassing sign." I was fully aware of the consequences, but it might be worth the risk. My wings trembled with excitement and my heart pounded apprehensively like a jungle drum.

The cool gust of wind caught me, nearly blowing me over, sending me catapulting across the lawn. An updraft pushed me from the left.

Dried and broken leaves leapfrogged back and forth with each soft gust of wind, beckoning me to come closer, daring me to peep in the windows.

As if driven by an unseen hand, stealthily moving closer, I zoomed in and hung upside down in the murky shadows near a downstairs window.

Masquerades were the costume of choice.

Butlers dressed in tiny black suits and ties with silver trays resting upon their right arms were descending the winding, wooden staircases. Their shoes were spit-polished and shiny.

Dancers were twirling and bobbing rhythmically to the beat of haunting music in the large ballroom to the left of the window. Tall, thin skeletons swayed stiffly to the cadence of the masqueraded orchestra.

Little Green Goblins, their ears twitching, but tuned to all the conversations in the room, ravenously filled their plates from the buffet table. White, gauzy ghosts drifted and swayed, clasping and unclasping hands as they moved, swirling around the crystal chandeliers. Witches, clad in black from head to toe, congregated around an enormous black pot, with the plumpest witch stirring the steamy broth. Smoke filled the air, and their cackles could be heard above the music in the night air.

As I listened, the bubbly pot cried my name, "Come closer. Join me!"

Was it actually speaking in an audible voice? What was inside the pot? Shivers crept up and down my spine.

The cool, thin breeze caught the fur on the back of my head; I hung suspended in air, wings outstretched, mesmerized by the action within.

Perhaps I was tired; maybe there was something in my blood.

This place had been completely empty for years, no vehicles were ever in the driveway, yet tonight there were hundreds of masquerading dancers within. As I hung precariously upside down from the eaves, the action within held my attention.

I allowed myself to blow back-and-forth in the breeze, enraptured by the partiers within. It might have been hours; it had only been a few minutes.

As the hors d'oeuvres were served, ghostly music wafted out into the night and two miniature goblins swung wildly from chandelier to chandelier – boots flying.

My pulse slowed. Thump. Thump. Thump. Tiny hammers in my heart pumped blood so quickly my wings began to quiver. My feet nearly lost their grip on the edge of the overhang.

Frozen in time, I remained transfixed upside down: watching, waiting, curious.

Gently, the breeze tugged at me again. Something brushed against my shoulder. Gasping, I turned to see another who resembled myself.

"What? Who?" I gasped. "You frightened me!"

She smiled. "Gotcha. I'm Dusty."

"I'm Epomops."

"I've always been intrigued by this dilapidated mansion," she mouthed. "Is that why you stopped, too?"

From behind her back, she pulled two large, colorfully sequined masks. "One for you and one for me. Join me?"

"Of course," I said, flipping right side up, and pulling the glamourous piece up to my face.

"Here is where the excitement begins," she giggled as she did several circles and a series of acrobatics until she landed, feet first on the top step of the mansion. As she did, her mask went up, and she reached up to ring the rusty doorbell.

Silently a rotund waiter in a black tuxedo opened the door and spoke gruffly, "Invitations."

"Sir, it appears that I've left them on my kitchen table."

"Never mind, I've got an extra one or two right here," he said dryly, pulling them from his coat pocket and thrusting them out for Dusty to hold. "You will need these. Your masquerades are exceptional. They are the best I've seen all evening. Authentic."

"Thank you. We diligently crafted them."

"Really?" I whispered as we entered the hall. "We're in our own skin. The only reason we could pull this off is because it is a masquerade party."

Dusty led the way, as if she knew every inch of the mansion – rushing past tall paintings of eloquent men and women of ages past. She swiped her hands reverently across the tapestry draped in the hallway.

In an upper room, there was an old chess board. A two-paned round mirror cast an image of four of us as we played chess late into the evening.

"Checkmate." Her laughter rang out inside the room.

"Of course," I sighed. "It has been years since I played chess with my grandfather. My skills are rusty, to say the least."

"It's fine," she laughed. "There are so many other ways to skin a cat. Come on! It's time to explore!"

She led me back downstairs, past the potted plants, and into the library. Three mummies wrapped in disintegrating linen were having a heated discussion about dance steps as they sat stiffly in the overstuffed chairs.

"I can do the two step so much better than you."

"Put your boots on and let's see!"

"Come on," she whispered, "unless you want to get pulled into an argument, the hallway library calls."

Shelves and shelves of dusty, well-worn books lined the walls – Emerson, Dickens, and Monroe.

"Time for a quick reading break?" I gasped. "Oh, the things we could read."

"Maybe next time," she smiled, pulling on my wing.

Masqueraders were in every room enjoying the opportunity to mingle and revel in the mansion.

As the hands on the clock struck midnight, my backside brushed gently against the light switch in the hallway.

The great room went dark. Screams erupted and an eerie silence filled the air. Reaching behind me, Dusty flipped the switch back on it and revealed a dismal sight.

All the masqueraders had turned to dust; masks and elegant costumes lay on the floor in heaps. Beside the door were the remnants of the rotund butler's uniform, two tickets, a pair of black shiny shoes, and a silver tray. Both chandeliers fell from the ceiling simultaneously with a thunderous crash sending dust particles flying toward our upturned faces.

As the glass shattered, Dusty grabbed my wing and pulled me toward the door, "Close call."

"Curiosity nearly killed the cat!" I groaned as we raced past where the butler had once been, past the broken door, out into the heavy darkness.

The rusty gate creaked on its hinges. Our hearts, beating like hammers, made pounding noises.

A gentle breeze blew us upward, and we zoomed off – our silhouettes outlined by the moon.

"The night is still young and there is another mansion down the road," Dusty smiled and winked.

"Thanks for the adventure, but I've got to head home to my lab," I laughed.

"Thanks for the adventure, Epomops. I've always been curious."

"Now you know," I said, as we dipped and rose with the wind.

The lights were strangely absent the following evening as I flew past the Gothic Mansion, but once more the leaves danced across the lawn daring me to cross over into its world.

Shelle Renae is the author of the Iggy and Izzy Series, Marshmallow Superhero Series, and It is In series. A professional Literacy Coach (and former teacher of 25 plus years) by day, novelist by night, she received her Bachelor of Science at Bemidji State University and her masters of Curriculum and Instruction from Chapman University in California. A Minnesota native, she is a lover of family, writing stories, photography, rollerblading, traveling, and beaches. Currently she resides in California, most likely multi-tasking. Visit her online at: https://www.shellerenae.com/

SPLIT SEQUENCE HAIKU

CHRISTINE L. VILLA, SUSAN BETH FURST, & CLAIRE VOGEL CAMARGO

NCPA is pleased to present a fairly new type poetry: a **Split Sequence Haiku**, one that many of our readers may have never seen before, so a definition, a description, and a "blurb" follows.

Definition: A 12-line linked haiku form, plus title, written solo or collaboratively.

Simple description: A sequence is started by the poet splitting the 3-line haiku into 3 separate lines, then writing a haiku for each line. If it's a collaboration with another poet, each poet alternates in writing the haiku, distinguished by one poet writing in plain text, *the other in italics*.

Each split sequence poem interlaces sprouting haiku inside a seed haiku, which leaves the reader thinking, dreaming, reminiscing, emoting, and wanting, much, much more. – **Michael H. Lester, haiku and tanka poet**

This form of poetry was invented by Peter Jastermsky in 2017. More detailed information can be found on Google.

* * *

The following three poems, written by two new NCPA members: Claire Vogel Camargo from Texas, and Susan Beth Furst in Virginia, will be grouped together. Each author collaborates with long-time NCPA member, Christine L. Villa from California.

* * *

HOLIDAY BLUES
Christine L. Villa, California (plain text)
Claire Vogel Camargo, Texas (in italics)

Christmas night

> *holiday movies*
> *everyone smiles*
> *around the tree*

blinking lights

> Covid lockdown
> stars in the sky
> unmasked

of the ambulance

> *we all gather*
> *for a family feast*
> *his shortness of breath*

* * *

PAPER MOONS
Christine L. Villa, California (plain text)
Susan Beth Furst, Virginia (in italics)

Chinese New Year

dragon dance
we paint the town
red

a cloud of smoke

hunting

for candies and tangerines
swinging lanterns

from a firecracker

cellophane wrappers
all that's left
of children's dreams

*   *   *

DROWNING THE SHAMROCK
Christine L. Villa, California (plain text)
Susan Beth Furst, Virginia (in italics)

even the river

   parade
   a cold March wind
   plays with the band

a leprechaun green

   last shot of whisky
   waking up with a man
   in a shamrock shirt

St. Patrick's Day

   rainbow's end
   still searching for
   the pot of gold

SANTA'S MAGICAL VISIT

YVONNE WHALEN

There was never a year where Christmas was not special. My parents always ensured it was a day we could keep with us forever. There is one Christmas though that was extra magical. It started on Christmas Eve 1972.

"Kids, hurry! Come see quickly," Mom yelled excitedly.

My younger sister, brother, and I ran from the various rooms to see what was going on. As we made it to the living room, all at the same time, we saw our mother standing at the window with the drapes pulled aside. Her eyes sparkled as her smile grew from ear to ear.

"Come, look, hurry. It's Santa! He's almost here," Mom said as she pulled each of us to the window.

You could've heard a pin drop as each of us kids watched in silence, watched in awe as a string of lights moved across the night sky. The blinking red light at the front convinced us that Rudolph was leading the reindeers for Santa; just like in the movies.

Suddenly, our mother dropped the drapes and clapped her hands, her smile wide, as she told us we needed to get to bed quickly.

"Santa will soon be here," Mom said, her eyes holding that hint of glee of a person with a secret. "But he won't come if you don't go to sleep."

Mom's smile turned to the warmth only a mother can show as she told us she loved us and wished us sweet dreams.

Of course, there was no way we could sleep. We were too excited. At that time, we shared a bedroom and if my mother was listening at the door, she would've heard us whisper to each other excitedly that Santa was coming, and would have heard our guesses as to what he would bring us.

As we continued to whisper our guesses, an extremely loud thump rang out on the roof above our heads. The thump was followed by the unmistakable sound of jingle bells. At first, it was startling, but then we excitedly whispered that Santa was at our house. There were several more thumps across the roof and the jingle bells never stopped ringing.

After a few minutes, we could hear the jingle bells in the living room. At this point, we were all sitting up in bed listening to the commotion. Then, we heard the jingle bells come down the hallway, and getting louder, until they stopped at our bedroom door. The three of us suddenly laid down and pretended we were sleeping. We could hear the door crack open a little bit as if someone was checking on us.

I dared not move. I was so excited I could barely breathe. After a few moments that felt like years, the door closed. The jingle bells moved back into the living room where we could hear items being moved around.

We sat up once again, listening to what was happening in the living room. Soon, all was quiet. But, not for long. Jingle bells rang and hooves thumped and stomped across the roof.

Just as suddenly as it started, it was over. Santa came and left to visit the next house. Of course, we were too excited to stay in bed. We each got up and tiptoed to the bedroom door. We bravely continued down the hall to the living room. I remember we just stared in awe. Our Christmas tree was lit, and we had presents! We also noticed the plate of cookies that we had left for Santa was empty.

We ran to our mother's room yelling and hollering that Santa had come. All of us jumped on her bed, wanting to wake her. She sat up laughing and listened intently to our excited glee, all the while hugging us – or trying to.

Knowing she couldn't contain us for long, Mom said we should go see what Santa brought us. Of course, not waiting for her to change her mind, we jumped off the bed and ran back to the living room, our mother right behind us, laughing.

Looking back now, I could tell Mom enjoyed our excitement. She had us all sit down around the tree as she began pulling packages from under it and handing them out. We never hesitated; we began ripping the paper off.

After a while of playing with our gifts, Mom ushered us back to bed. She made it clear that when we got up in the morning, we could play with our presents some more. When morning came, we were excited all over again. But this Christmas morning we didn't have to wake up our mother to open anything. We had already opened them. We spent all morning and the rest of that day playing with our presents and talking about Santa's visit.

It's 2021 and I'm now grown, with adult kids of my own. I remember my kids often asking me when they were little if I believed in Santa. With a sparkle and a smile, I always told them I did. And I will never forget the magic and excitement of my own special Santa visit.

Yvonne enjoyed a fulfilling 25-year career as a Funeral Director, retiring in May 2019. She garnered a BS in Management and completed her MBA in Management and Strategy and continued to certify as a Six Sigma Black Belt Professional (SSBBP); in addition to the industry licensing, she procured in Death Care. In 2020 she ventured into the publishing world by starting her own eBook publishing business, The Pyrateheart Press. Visit her website at www.pyrateheartpress.com.

Yvonne has 3 boys, loves to travel and has traveled extensively the continental United States and hopes to go to Belize in the future.

A resident of Sacramento, California Yvonne enjoys membership in various organizations, such as, the National Association of Women Business Owners, the National Notary Association, the North Sacramento Chamber of Commerce, the North Sacramento Rotary Club and the Placer Women's Network where she is also a 2021 Board Member.

TURKEY WINDSTORM,
NOVEMBER 24, 1983

CAROLYN RADMANOVICH

Inside my cozy condo in Edmonds, Washington, I slid the stout Thanksgiving turkey into the preheated oven. The wind blasted the Ponderosa pines outside, and the plump rain pummeled the windows. Suddenly, a poof echoed throughout the kitchen as the lights went out and the TV went silent.

"Powers out," I yelled to the family. "Now, what are we going to do about dinner?" Unbeknownst to us, the power had gone out for much of the Puget Sound area, ruining many turkey dinners.

My new sweetheart, Richard, who had driven up from the Bay Area, a thousand miles away, to spend this special holiday with us, put his hand up to quell my concern. "Never fear," he said. "Being from the mountains of Boulder Creek, I have plenty of experience with power outages."

Richard and I met two months earlier in Santa Cruz at my niece's wedding. He was neighbors and best friends with my sister and brother-in-law. Since their daughter was getting married, they had invited him, never thinking of introducing us two single people. I flew down from Seattle, not knowing how the trip would impact my life, for I would be meeting my future husband.

After my niece's wedding, we ended up sitting at the same table, so we introduced ourselves. There was an instant bond the moment we met. Since he had learned from my sister that I was a meditator, he offered to loan me a spiritual book. I asked, "How will I return it?" He answered, "I'll drive up and get it." He came to claim the book two weeks later and promptly forgot about it when he enfolded me in his arms at my doorway.

The second time he visited was our first Thanksgiving together. I was thrilled to have his company. On his first trip, he had proven himself a worthy contender for my wary sons, ages 11 and 13. To win them over, he had taken them to the Seattle Center in his Alpha Romeo sports car, played games in the arcade, and won them giant stuffed animals. Later that week, all dreamy-eyed, they had approached saying they had talked it over and decided they wanted me to marry Richard. That would come to pass, but not quite as soon as they expected.

Hearing my complaint about a raw turkey for dinner, Richard asked, "Do you have a barbecue?"

"Yes, I have a tiny Smokey Joe."

"Perfect," he said as he sliced a chunk off the turkey. "We'll cook the breast. There will be plenty for us, including those two ravenous beasts." His smile broadened across his handsome face, framed by his well-groomed goatee.

My heart swelled at his taking decisive action. He was quite the resilient man. Besides, my kids liked him and his sense of humor.

He opened the slider and went onto the patio, the wind blowing his thick dark-brown hair back. I glanced at him dropping coal into the Smokey Joe.

While he was busy lighting the coals, I put more logs into the black metallic freestanding fireplace that sat at one end of the living room. I prepared the Russet potatoes, wrapping them in aluminum foil after dousing them with olive oil, salt, and pepper. The potatoes roasted in the fireplace and the flames reflected off the kids' faces as they sat on the floor playing Monopoly.

After Richard finished getting the coals lit and putting the turkey in the barbecue, he came inside. The resultant wind blew some of our Monopoly pieces and cards around the room, but we found everything, and he joined us for a new game. When I sat cross-legged by the fire, our cat sat on my lap and purred, happy to be joining in the fun. Richard sat to my right and scratched the cat's head.

When the turkey was done, Richard brought it to the

kitchen and tented it with foil for a few minutes. I took out the two salads I had prepared earlier that morning. A raspberry Jell-o salad with fruit and a green salad with tomatoes were a great addition. I put the rolls wrapped in foil on the coals of the fireplace and removed the baked potatoes. After the table was set, the turkey sliced, and the food displayed, we had a marvelous dinner by candlelight.

Being an adventurer, I suggested we stack the dishes in the sink and then drive to Green Lake for a walk. The kids were enthused, and we convinced Richard, who seemed reluctant to drive in a storm. On the twenty-minute drive, we observed the street lights bouncing like children at a party. Branches and leaves filled the streets, but we were able to get through on the main thoroughfares. The storm had caused havoc with trees leaning on fences and rooftops.

When we arrived, Green Lake was close to being deserted. What crazy people would go out on a day like this? The wind roared in our ears when we got out of the car. Ski hats protected our hair from flapping out of control. It was difficult to walk upright, so we angled our bodies into the wind, then playfully leaned backward to see how far we could go without falling over.

The stratocumulus clouds scudded across the sky, and the trees did a crazy dance. The yellow cottonwoods tossed their leaves onto the trail. Redwood branches bowed, almost touching the ground. Our eyes grew big at the sounds of branches popping off alders and slamming onto the ground. Slender dogwoods broke off at the base. Ponderosa pines dropped their cones. A black walnut dropped a ten-foot-long branch across the trail, and we jumped over it, giddy at being part of this incredible storm. We were happy to have indulged ourselves in this rare event, enthused to have fellow adventurers for company.

When we arrived back at the condo, we ate pumpkin pie and whipped cream. Afterward, Richard and I held hands as we settled onto the couch for storytelling by flickering candlelight. Snug in the condo as the storm continued pounding the windows with torrential gusts of moisture-laden wind, we knew the next day would be even more spectacular. The kids would stay at their dad's for the weekend, and we were headed to a Marrowstone Island cabin to be alone during the tail-end of the storm.

Instead of this gale creating a catastrophe, we turned it into an event never to be forgotten. This would be my favorite Thanksgiving etched into my memory. There would be other momentous occasions, but none as heart-warming.

 Fascinated by the wild west, Carolyn Radmanovich earned a history degree from San Jose State University. After a near-drowning incident on the Russian River, she felt compelled to write her first book, *The Shape-Shifter's Wife*, about an anthropologist, Angelica, who time travels to the California gold rush of 1848 and meets a handsome Frenchman. This book won the 2018 Independent Book Awards for Visionary Fiction. The sequel, *The Gypsy's Warning*, focuses on the sister, Heather, who time travels to find Angelica. Carolyn's short stories, *Tex's Dream* and *Frenchie – A Love Story*, were included in the NCPA anthologies, *Birds of a Feather* and More Birds of a Feather, along with several others. The California Writers Club selected her short story, *Prod*, for second place in the 2019 Memoir Contest. Carolyn lives in Lincoln, California, with her husband and cat, Tex. Check her website at www.CarolynRadmanovich.com.

THE SANTA FE SPECIAL
SUSAN BETH FURST

*__Haiku__ is a three-line, beautifully descriptive, form of poetry, intended to be read in one breath. The Academy of American Poets asserts, *"As the form evolved, many...rules – including the 5-7-5 practice – have routinely been broken..."* Possibly the three-line has been, also.

Sugar-plum dreams...
The Santa Fe Special
Thunders through Plasticville

(__Explanation for non-poetry readers:__ This one is based on personal memories. We had a train under our Christmas tree – an old Lionel, the Santa Fe Special. It would go round the tree. We had a village too. It was a very popular and now a collectable dime store item. The trade name was Plasticville. The sugar plum dreams is a clue that it is Christmas.)

*   *   *

HALLOWEEN MOON
SUSAN BETH FURST

the mummy unwinds
Halloween moon

(__Explanation for non-poetry readers:__ The Halloween haiku is just a play on words. The mummy unwinds ... relaxes, or literally unwinds ... It can be read both ways. What makes it interesting is the use of the word moon. Moon is a season word used in haiku. It is often overdone. So, a sort of tongue in cheek, if you read the poem literally you might see the mummy's "moon". Or it could be a fall moon, a Halloween moon.)

THE MAGIC OF CHRISTMAS EVE
BOB IRELAN

Nowadays the promotions for Christmas start several weeks before Thanksgiving. I don't believe I will ever get comfortable with that.

As a little boy, Christmas excitement didn't really begin for me until early-to-mid-December. By then I had figured out what I hoped Santa Claus might bring. But I wasn't totally possessed by the proximity of the holiday. That would occur the 20th or so when Christmas vacation began.

Looking back, I guess I was insulated from a lot of the hoopla because I lived "out in the country." Our address was R.F.D. #1, Silver Spring, Maryland. "R.F.D" is an abbreviation for "Rural Free Delivery," and the then-small city of Silver Spring was seven or eight miles away.

Our white frame house seemed big, but by today's standard, it was not. It fronted on a two-lane road (now a four-lane thoroughfare) and was bordered by one farm in the back, another on one side, and woodlands on the other. The farms and woodlands are long gone, replaced mostly by large homes on spacious lots. But, wonder of wonders, our 85-year-old house still stands, separated a bit from the newer ones and looking somewhat worse for wear.

My closest childhood friend, Roger Curtis, lived on a farm a half-mile away. When not in school, we would spend most days at either his house or mine. If I did not return home for lunch, my mother assumed Roger's mother was feeding me, and vice versa. Depending on the season, playtime was spent bike riding, sledding, fishing, skinny dipping at our favorite swimming hole, or rearranging bales of hay to create a network of tunnels.

Roger's farm had a variety of livestock whereas we had only chickens, a few turkeys and ducks, and several rabbits.

A favorite springtime tradition was venturing into the woods to look for box turtles as they emerged after a winter of hibernation.

We shared party-line telephone service with several other families. We knew some neighbors listened in at least occasionally. We did not. If there was an emergency or if a neighbor had tied up the line for what seemed like hours, we'd ask to interrupt and place a brief call. Back then, phones didn't have buttons or dials, and they were wired firmly to the wall. If you wanted to call someone, you picked up the receiver and asked the operator to connect you to whatever number you wanted. After all those years, I still remember our phone number, Kensington 249 J.

We got our news from the newspaper and radio. Milk was delivered to the front porch. Holmes Bakery ("Holmes to Homes" was its slogan) delivered bread and offered an assortment of baked goods twice a week.

Personal safety wasn't a concern. Our exposure to crime was listening to *This Is Your FBI* on the radio or viewing a *Boston Blackie* or *Charlie Chan* feature at the Seco Theatre in Silver Spring.

We did have a father and son duo of drunks who, especially on weekend evenings, staggered down the darkened road after too many beers at Hull's store. Both were harmless, and local drivers watched out for them so as not to run them down.

Birthdays brought a present or two; Christmas, three, possibly four. My favorites included cowboy boots, a Roadmaster bicycle, and books – especially ones about cowboys and Indians.

Maybe living in a relatively pastoral setting served to perpetuate Christmas traditions my parents had enjoyed when they were children. I had no reason to believe that how we celebrated and when we celebrated was much different from the practices of others.

I'm not sure at what age I figured out Mom and Dad were providing my Christmas gifts. I think I continued to believe in Santa longer than most of my childhood friends. I may have had some doubts, but I didn't want to risk not believing. What if there were consequences?

My parents went above and beyond when it came to the logistics of Christmas. While other families put their Christmas tree up maybe a week or ten days prior to the 25th, we didn't. We would, with permission of course, cut a tree from one or another of the neighbors' farmland or woods on, say, the 22nd or 23rd of December and lay it on the side porch. Then, magically, Santa would somehow find the time to haul the tree in the house, stand it up, and decorate it after my brother and I went to bed on Christmas Eve.

I never believed Santa came down our chimney. Clearly, the opening was too small. So, of course, we made sure to leave the door to the porch unlocked.

I always marveled at the precise way in which the lights, with multi-colored foil reflectors attached behind them, were distributed throughout the tree. Also, how the tinsel hung so perfectly. Santa was such a perfectionist. If that wasn't enough, he also found time to set up our electric train set, complete with mountainous terrain, a tunnel and bridge.

How could he do all this and still deliver presents to everyone else around the world? I didn't know. I didn't want to know. I just believed.

Neither did I question how tired my parents appeared when my brother and I awakened them at 5:00 or 6:00 Christmas morning, pleading to go into the living room to see what Santa had brought. (My brother was three years older than I, but most likely on orders from my parents, didn't blow Santa's cover prematurely.)

Years later, as a young adult with our first child on the way, I told my wife about my family's tradition of waiting until Christmas Eve to set up our tree. Her response was a look of disbelief. That was all it took. A new tradition began. Our tree would go up a couple of weeks before Christmas.

Since then, putting up the tree and other decorations has begun even earlier, like the first week of December (and still I lag behind many of my friends).

As I revisit my childhood memories, I am reminded of all the loving things my parents did for me. Near the top of this lengthy list is the Herculean effort they put forth on those early Christmas Eves to preserve a little boy's belief in Santa Claus and his magical ability to accomplish so much for so many in a single night.

Following 10 years of newspaper and magazine reporting and editing, including stints at The Wall Street Journal and Nation's Business magazine in Washington, DC, Bob Irelan spent 32 years managing public relations for a Fortune 500 family of companies.

In retirement, he taught a public relations course for two years at University of the Pacific and for five years at University of California, Davis, Extension.

Bob is the author of two novels. The first, *Angel's Truth – One Teenager's Quest for Justice*, was published in 2018 and took second place in Fiction at NCPA's 25th Annual Book Awards. The second, *Justifiable – Murder in the Mountain State*, was published in September 2020.

His short stories are among those included in these NCPA anthologies: *Birds of a Feather, More Birds of a Feather, and Destination: The World, Volumes One and Two*. He lives with his cat, Bai, in Rancho Murieta, California.

CELEBRATE

JUDITH VAUGHAN

L ight filters through Glenda's still-closed eyelids as she slowly awakens. She's dreaming it's her birthday. Her mother always places presents for her on the bedside table the night before. She finds them just as she wakes up. She gets her quarter from the tooth fairy the same way.

She savors the moment knowing that as soon as she opens her eyes, she'll see the table stacked with four or five presents wrapped in paper printed with bold stripes or cake and candles. She'll try to guess their content. Hefty books, regular in shape, give themselves away while small boxes only suggest. Glenda will shake one anticipating the jingle of a charm bracelet and sniff another for a whiff of Chanel.

She opens her eyes. No presents. Only the dusty reading light and the book she was reading last night meet her anticipatory smile that's crumbling even as she dives back under the covers.

"It's not your birthday, silly." A girlish voice scolds her. "There are no presents. It's your unbirthday and not a very good one at that."

Glenda opens one eye. A lanky girl with thick pale hair secured with a ribbon now stands in her room. She's wearing an old-fashioned dress with a starched, ruffled apron. Glenda recognizes her and throws off the quilt. It's Alice, of Wonderland fame, with a figure standing beside her.

Is the figure an egg or a man?

"Humpty," says Alice. "Where are your manners?"

The figure bows his head. "I see Glenda isn't dressed. I'll wait in the hall."

Glenda sees that he's a rotund egg, not a man. She recognizes Humpty Dumpty from his nursery rhyme. She pulls off her pajamas and puts on her jeans and a tee shirt. "Let's go to the breakfast bar and have some tea," she says, remembering that her guests are English.

"Brilliant," says Alice. "Humpty will eggsplain the concept of the unbirthday once we're settled with the tea."

Glenda leads the two into the kitchen. On the counter, she sets out souvenir mugs from San Francisco featuring the chocolate factory, the Golden Gate Bridge, and Alcatraz. She takes several boxes of tea bags out of the cupboard. Her guests watch rapt as she proceeds.

"Oh." She sees her guests are puzzled.

"Your teacups are odd," says Humpty. "A picture of a jail. Mine are much more delicate – with lilacs."

Alice says, "Where's your teakettle? Or your stove?"

"I'm going to heat the tea in my microwave," Glenda replies.

Alice touches it. "How will that work? It isn't even hot?"

"It's a modern machine. I'll show you in a minute. Pick your tea first. Would you like black tea, green tea, peach passion herb tea, or decaf...perhaps English Breakfast?"

The two nod vigorously.

Alice says, "I'll take English Breakfast though I don't understand the name. Our tea is from Ceylon and breakfast was hours ago. It's teatime now. But Teatime Tea would be redundant."

Glenda puts a teabag in each of the three souvenir mugs and then fills them at the tap. She puts the mugs into the microwave and sets a timer.

"Why is the tea in little net bags?" says Humpty.

When the timer dings, Glenda explains not just the teabags but the powdered sweetener and creamer with a minimum of comment, though her guests are still shaking their heads and she herself is finding the situation strange. The three sit down on the high stools of the kitchen bar.

"My goodness," says Humpty, "this stool is as precarious as the wall in Looking Glass Land." His eggy brow furrows. "I suspect the King's horses and all the King's men are far away. Please catch me, Glenda, if I fall."

Glenda is relieved when they sip the tea without

complaint and finally seem out of questions.

Alice kicks her legs against the bar stool. "The unbirthday was introduced into the English lexicon by Humpty Dumpty," says Alice like a proud mother. "The White Queen gave him an unbirthday present, a cravat—that's a tie to you, Glenda."

The giant egg bows slightly. "I argued its merits to Alice back in Looking Glass World. There are 364 days when you might get an unbirthday present and only one for a birthday present. There's the glory for you."

Glenda joins the conversation. "I get it, and every day that isn't the Fourth of July is the un-Fourth of July. And there are 364 un-Halloweens, too. No wonder we're annoyed with the fireworks on the wrong day. And how our waistlines suffer with the candy!"

Humpty shakes his head. "You Americans! You don't have tea in the parlor, and there isn't any cream or sugar. You don't understand."

"Wait," says Alice. "Other un-holidays shouldn't be celebrated. And not every unbirthday. Our agendas would be overwhelmed, and we'd soon be bored of even the nicest gifts."

She takes a white card from the pocket of her apron. "Here's the White Queen's guide:

When to Celebrate a Friend's Unbirthday
    By the White Queen
You forgot their real birthday. It'll relieve your guilt.
You see the perfect gift for them and their birthday's not for months.
You appreciate them and your feelings demand an outlet.
They give you a gift, and it turns out it's your unbirthday."

Glenda smiles. "Thank you, Alice and Humpty Dumpty. I will surely celebrate someone's unbirthday soon."

Alice and Humpty are fading slowly away as they all return to Glenda's bedroom. Alice waves. She's as pale as the illustrations printed in black and white in the book on Glenda's bedside table, Through the Looking Glass.

"A very happy unbirthday to you." They all sing to Glenda.

Glenda opens the Victorian box that has just appeared. Alice's white hair ribbon is folded back and forth on itself like ribbon candy. Glenda has found her unbirthday present.

Judy Vaughan grew up in Northern New Mexico surrounded by sacred mountains and engrossed in the lives of horses and other animals. She has composed stories since childhood, and began to hone the craft of writing after forty years practicing neurology. She lives in Elk Grove, California, and writes with Elk Grove Writers and Artists. She has published an award winning New Mexico memoir, *Strawberry Roan*. Her stories have placed in short story contests and have been published in NCPA Anthologies. *Celebrate* began when Judy mixed a memory with a scene from Lewis Carroll's Through the Looking Glass.

WISHES

SUSAN BETH FURST
Flash Fiction

There are seven buttercream roses on the top of Mr. O'Leary's cake. I have my eye on the pink one in the middle. Gramma lights the candles, and I cross my fingers so the roses won't melt.

"Call the fire department," Pap yells.

I watch as one of Mr. O'Leary's ears start to twitch. Pap says Mr. O'Leary is a leprechaun. I think he just likes to wear green.

"Make a wish," Gramma chortles.

Mr. O'Leary looks at Gramma and smiles. His stomach grows two sizes as he sucks all the air from the room. He huffs and puffs until he blows out every candle except one, which he finishes off with a sloppy wet whoosh.

"Who wants cake?" Gramma asks.

Mom covers her mouth and shakes her head. Aunt Louise stares intently at her feet. Pap's face turns the color of an overripe tomato. Gramma takes a sip of her Pepsi.

"I want the piece in the middle," I say as I stick my finger in the icing. I get a bowl of ice cream instead.

Mr. O'Leary is busy eating his second piece of cake.

"Crazy like a fox," Pap says under his breath.

Gramma boxes up the rest of the cake for Mr. O'Leary to take home. She reminds Pap to use the emergency brake when he drops off Mr. O'Leary.

"Remember what happened last time, Sunny; it was a miracle that Mr. O'Leary didn't roll down the hill and into the ravine."

Pap snorts as he walks out the front door to warm up the car.

Gramma helps Mr. O'Leary with his green scarf. I notice the shamrocks on his socks as he climbs into the back seat.

I watch the taillights disappear as Pap drives slowly up the hill.

While everyone is looking for their coats, I sneak off to the kitchen where I hid the rose, the pink one in the middle. I'm sure Mr. O'Leary will never miss it.

A TRADITIONAL POLISH CHRISTMAS

A.K. BUCKROTH

This story will help explain and describe a long-lost traditional Polish dinner that is reverently celebrated on Christmas Eve.

Wigilia, pronounced "*Vigilia*," (from the Latin word *vigil* as in to watch or observe) is the Polish word expressing a formal, traditional dinner and its preparations the night before Christmas. Having begun in the 10th century, its familiarity has waned through the decades.

However, I continue to prepare and participate in this happy event taught to me by my mother, a descendant of Polish immigrants.

The word and preparatory processes stem from an ancient Polish cliché: "A guest in the home is God in the home." It is a meatless meal, no doubt the result of a long-time church mandate that a strict fast and abstinence be observed on this day before Christmas.

My immediate family strictly adhered to this dictate.

As the story goes, when the first star appears in the Eastern sky on December 24th, a Polish family gathers at the dinner table for the Wigilia Supper, a feast to commemorate the birth of the God Child. In farm homes, sheaves of grain, tied with colored ribbons, are placed in the corners of the room with a silent prayer for a good harvest in the next season.

Although not a farmer — or a farmer's wife by any means — hanging in one corner of our kitchen is a small bundle of hay, 10" x 5", tied together with one red and one white ribbon, the colors of Poland. It signifies prosperity. As a prayerful woman, my silent prayers are steady and steadfast on a daily basis for health and happiness. It signifies prosperity.

Legend and tradition continue and for this special dinner, a thin layer of hay is spread on the dinner table under a white tablecloth in memory of the God Child in the manger.

A bale of hay is rather large, and I only require a smidgeon, but having to purchase a whole bale to accomplish this task, finding useful techniques for it are scarce, so I use the remainder to line our dog's house for his comfort, along with spreading hay in the garden as mulch.

Before sitting down to the dinner table, the breaking of a traditional thin wafer made of flour and water, called *Oplatek* (pronounced "*opwatek*"), is shared with all participants. Each thin unleavened wafer, like the altar bread in church, is stamped with the figures of the God Child, the Blessed Mary, and the Holy Angels. Its taste is just like the Holy Communion host given during a Catholic Mass. Each participant breaks a piece of this bread, and exchanges good wishes to all who are present. It is known as the Bread of Love.

The Supper itself greatly differs from other evening meals in that the number of courses is fixed at seven, nine or eleven; and in no case must there be an odd number of people at the table. Otherwise — as has been told to me — some of the feasters would not live to see another Christmas! A lighted candle in a window symbolizes the hope that the God Child, in the form of a stranger, may come to share your *Wigilia* Supper, and an extra place is set at the table for the expectant guest.

However, this part of the tradition has been halted due to unexpected and possibly frightening mishaps of the present times, so I have never left a lighted candle in any window to attract unwanted attention! During my *Wigilia* dinners, an extra place continues to be set for loved ones who have passed away.

Christmas trees are very popular in Poland. In the large houses in the cities, they are placed on the floor or the table; in the villages, they are hung from the ceiling, all decorated with apples, nuts, candies and many small toys made out of blown eggs, colored paper and straw. It is supposed that the gifts were brought by an angel, since their St. Nicholas had visited the children on December sixth. An old Christmas carol is sung and then the gifts are opened. More carols follow and there is great joy and merriment.

Never having seen a pine tree hanging from a ceiling, I cannot imagine or even visualize such a thing. It would be my luck that one or more of the decorations would fall off and hit me on the noggin!

Polish carols, *Kolendy*, are very numerous and beautiful, sung in any language.

Year after year as a child brought up in a Polish school, Polish church, by a Polish mother and her siblings, I have sung the *Pasterka* (Shepherds' Watch) at Midnight Masses along with numerous other Christmas songs in Polish.

It is a popular belief in Poland's villages that while the congregation is praying, peace descends on the snow-clad sleeping earth, and during this holy night, the humble companions of men, the domestic animals, assume voices; but only the innocent may hear them.

Christmas Day is spent in rest, prayer and with visits to various members of the family, and from Christmas Eve until the Twelfth Night, boys trudge from village to village with an illuminated star in a ranting depiction, King Herod among them, to sing carols. Sometimes they walk through towns in expectation of more generous gifts. In some districts, the boys carry puppet shows called *szopki* (pronounced shop-key), that are built like little houses with two towers, open in the front where a small crib is set and where marionettes sing their dialogue. During the Christmas season, the theaters give special Christmas performances.

On the feast of Epiphany, the priest and the organist have been known to visit homes, bless them and write over doors the initials of the Three Wise Men (KMB) in the belief that this will spare the occupants misfortune.

The Christmas season closes on February second, *Candlemas Day*. On that day, people carry candles to church and have them blessed for use in their homes during storms, sickness and death.

My family, with my mother at the helm, did part take in

this belief.

Among the Poles, wherever they are, the most beloved and beautiful of all their traditional festivities is that of Christmas Eve. In the words of their forefathers, who called the Christmas Days *Gody*, it is to them a time of good will, love, harmony, forgiveness, and peace.

Seven, nine and eleven-course suppers were served in some homes, and in some parts of Poland a twelve-course meal was typical.

Suggested Christmas Eve, Wigilia, Supper Menus:

Seven Courses
Herring and pickled mushrooms; clear *barszcz* (boiled beet broth) with Mushroom Pierogi U*szka* (small dumplings filled with minced meat and or mushrooms); pike (freshwater fish) with horseradish sauce; baked sauerkraut with yellow peas; fried fish with lemon rings; dried fruit compote; pastries, coffee, nuts and candies.

Nine Courses
Pickled herring and boiled potatoes; mushroom soup; *pierogis*, an absolute favorite, are similar to Italian raviolis but stuffed with fried cabbage and/or farmer's cheese; baked lake trout; baked sauerkraut with yellow peas; fish in aspic and potato salad; rice ring with creamed shrimp; jellied compote; pastries, coffee, nuts and candies.

Eleven Courses
Appetizers: pickled herring, individual salads; *pierogis* with mushrooms and browned butter; creamed fish soup with dumplings; pike fillets baked with cream; baked sauerkraut and mushrooms; pike in sauce; cauliflower with a crumb and butter topping; fried fresh salmon and potatoes with tomato sauce; prune compote; poppy seed cake; nut pudding; pastries, coffee, nuts and candies.

* * *

I spent hours researching members of the Polanie Club, which was established in 1948 after World War II to gather and preserve Polish culture and traditions in America. The Club members would offer self-help and mutual aid to each other and to other recent Polish immigrants, providing entertainment through Polish history, and traditions including Polish music to fulfill the social needs of its members. My mother and her family were upholding members throughout my childhood.

There existed the need to preserve some of the best Polish recipes in America. The Polish immigration movement to America did not reach its peak until early in the nineteenth century. This migration lasted until the restricting laws were passed in 1915, and many good cooks who have come from Poland are still among us.

On the shelves of many of the libraries are Polish cookbooks yellowing with age, sent to the United States when there was an exchange of free thought between Poland and other countries. One book specifically written and originally published for Americans in 1948, *Treasured Polish Recipes*, by Polanie Club Member, Irene Jasinski, edited by fellow club member Marie Sokolowski, is the result of research into these precious, old records. They provide invaluable help from good Polish cooks and contain contributions of cherished recipes and cooperative help of all the Polanie Club members.

*   *   *

I especially enjoy the following quote about measuring ingredients from that book, in its 11th printing in 1967: *"We have chosen food recipes available everywhere in America, yet we have been tested. We found many that directed the use of 'enough flour to make a still dough' or 'enough milk to make a pouring batter.' Such recipes were carefully tried and the 'unmeasured' ingredients were carefully measured and made part of the recipes in standard measures common in America."*

A.K. Buckroth, is presently a member of the Northern California Publishers and Authors (NCPA) organization, the Sacramento Suburban Writers Club (SSWC), and the San Joaquin Valley Writers (SJVW).

Once obtaining a Master's Degree from the University of Phoenix, she gained the empowerment and knowledge to write her first book. Known as a "Professional Diabetic" Ms. Buckroth has maintained more than six decades with this disease. Read it all in *My Diabetic Soul - An Autobiography* Revised Edition © 2018 which brought her numerous awards. She is also responsible for three other books: *Me and My Dog Named Money*, a child's story of diabetes (Revised © 2019), *Me & My Money Too,* Book Two (Revised © 2019), and *Kisses for Cash... T1D meets T2D,* Book Three © 2016 which received an NCPA award. Available via Amazon, Kindle, Nook, Smashwords and Audio.com among others. More information via www.mydiabeticsoul.com and #buckroth.

PHILIPPINE DEBUT: A RIGHT OF PASSAGE TO ADULTHOOD

CHRISTINE "CHRISSI" L. VILLA

In the Philippines, many young girls dream of having their grand 18th birthday celebration, or debut, a significant step into the world of adulthood. I was one of those girls, after having just attended an elaborate one.

I was so thrilled when my father announced I was going to have my debut at one of the five-star hotels in Manila, but I was anxious about how to plan it. Since my mother passed away when I was eight, I had no reliable full-grown woman to plan it with me. I was also the next debutante in line among my friends, so I couldn't get ideas from any of my peers. At that time, I also didn't know what an event planner was. Maybe, if I had one, it could have been a more organized and memorable celebration.

Before I share how a traditional debut is celebrated in the Philippines and how mine turned out, let me tell you where it originated. The tradition of the debut is said to have been derived from the Spanish tradition, Quinceanera, a coming-of-age celebration when a girl turns fifteen. After the Spanish colonized the Philippines, the Filipinos adopted this tradition. First, it was a way for esteemed and affluent families to formally introduce their newly matured daughters to eligible bachelors. Then, from a marriage-oriented celebration, it evolved into a celebration of a girl's transition into a woman.

Most debuts, whether extravagant or not, follow these traditional rituals:

GUEST LIST – This depends on how much the parents' budget is, but will definitely include the whole family, close relatives, friends, and classmates.

Most of my relatives were at my debut: cousins, aunts, and maternal grandparents. I made sure I also invited my close friends and classmates, including the ones who I thought would liven up the dance floor. The rest of the guest list consisted of business associates invited by my father.

18 ROSES – While writing the guest list, the debutante makes sure she has included 18 pre-selected males who will give her a rose, then dance the waltz with her. Traditionally, it is the father who gives the first rose and has the first dance with the debutante while a suitor or boyfriend gives the last rose and has the last dance.

In my case, I didn't know anything about the 18 roses so I wasn't able to pre-select 18 males. I don't think I even knew 18 males I would have liked to dance with. During my party, my father surprised us all by dancing in the middle of the ballroom and asking me to dance with him, but it wasn't a waltz! We were dancing to a '70s disco number, *Just Pick Me Up and Dance*. Then my grandfather danced the waltz with me. Those were precious moments I will never forget!

18 CANDLES – To be included in the guest list are the 18 female closest friends of the debutante. Each will light a candle, deliver a speech, and give well-wishes. The modern debuts have come up with other "18" variations such as 18 treasures and 18 shots. The 18 treasures represent things that are important to the debutante's journey into womanhood. Eighteen friends and relatives give her these gifts along with a short explanation as to why a certain gift was picked. The 18 shots refer to the toast and a drink, which is given by 18 friends and relatives, who will honor the lady of the night. Nowadays, the celebrant adds more twists to the "18" tradition, depending on her theme. Some new variations are the 18 sweets, 18 cupcakes, 18 chocolates, 18 shoes, 18 bags, 18 songs, 18 bills, 18 butterflies, and 18 sweet thoughts.

None of these happened during my debut. Just picking my partner and participants for my cotillion and practicing for hours on weekends fully occupied my mind.

THEME – The theme of the party determines the venue, decorations, debutante's gown, attire of guests, invitation, souvenirs, etc. Having this in mind, the debutante can let her personality shine.

I didn't have a theme at all. I didn't know who I was, what my interests were, or what I was passionate about. If I would have my debut all over again, it would be a fairy theme. I would dress up like a fairy, wearing sparkly make-up. The venue would be decorated with a rustic fairytale setting, consisting of flowers, tiny lights, and butterflies. Of course, there would be fairy dust and poetry sprinkled everywhere!

I remember my father struggling with how to come up with an invitation. As I mentioned earlier, I had only been invited to one debut at that time, so I showed him an example of an invitation. I also gave him a poem I wanted included in my invitation. The sample invitation had a poem, and it inspired me to write one for my own. Little did I know, my father would ask the printer to make an exact duplicate of the invitation I showed him. It was the exact color and size, font style, and design on the edge of the card. I was so embarrassed. I still haven't apologized to that friend, who, of course, wanted her invitation to be entirely her own style. I also didn't have the heart to tell my father I was disappointed, because he brought home a big stack of invitations to send out.

My souvenir was another thing that wasn't carefully planned. My father just picked out some small figurines with two or three random designs to give away, with a ribbon, and my name printed on them. Again, it wasn't what I expected, but I didn't know any better.

GOWN – Every girl's dream is to feel like a princess even for just one night. On her special 18th birthday, she gets the chance to make a grand entrance and to dance and laugh the night away.

Regarding my debut gown, I didn't have a say in it

either. My father assured me I didn't have anything to worry about because one of the top designers was going to make a gown for me for free. I was so excited, thinking that the designer would turn me into a beautiful grown-up lady.

On the day of my debut, while I was strutting around the house, my brother's friend spotted me and exclaimed, "Oh my gosh! You look like Thumbelina!"

At first, I thought it was a compliment, as one of my favorite picture books was Thumbelina, but with the guffaw and remark that followed, I knew there was something wrong. "You look much shorter!!!"

Hearing that, I looked in the mirror and knew he was right. The big ruffles around my neck and wrists, layers of silk from my waist to my toes, and the huge petticoat drowned my tiny frame.

PROGRAM – To ensure that the whole event is organized, an emcee or host should be assigned to facilitate the flow of the party. Often there is a prayer at the beginning of the ceremony, followed by video presentations, 18 roses, 18 candles, the grand cotillion waltz dance, speeches and other song and dance numbers.

I didn't think about this beforehand, so before we started our grand cotillion waltz dance, I had to push forward one of the participants to introduce the dance number. Fortunately, she saved the day, although you could tell she was nervous and unprepared.

COTILLION – A grand waltz performed by the debutante, her escort, and peers is rehearsed months before the celebration. This is a very significant part of a traditional debut.

I couldn't come up with a dance partner at that time since my boyfriend broke up with me six months earlier. I asked if he would still be my partner, but he turned me down and asked to be invited as a guest with a tag-along "friend". Of course, the "friend" was actually his new girlfriend. I could tell, because she clung to him like a monkey.

I ended up asking my older brother to be my dance

partner. I don't remember having a huge entourage dancing the waltz with me, but I can remember the hours of practice in our home during weekends with my closest friends and their partners to perfect the presentation. We also rehearsed a Cha-Cha dance number to the tune of Sergio Mendez's music.

Usually, the escort is a suitor or a boyfriend. I didn't have either, so I desperately asked a cousin to find me an escort. The day before my debut, a distant cousin, who nobody among my friends knew was a relative of mine, ended up as my escort. Luckily, he was a very good dancer, so we were able to quickly rehearse a solo disco swing dance for the party.

FOOD – Filipinos love food, so no matter what the budget is, food is always in abundance.

Thankfully, my father managed to have my debut celebration catered so everybody's gustatory cravings were satisfied. I even had an ice carving and a tall birthday cake. I remember asking my best friend to help me blow out the candles because I couldn't reach them. I still have, and cherish, the doll that was atop my birthday cake.

SOUND SYSTEM– A good sound system is necessary for an entertaining night.

My older brother and his friends took care of that. They made sure everybody got up and boogied. Most of the music played was '70s disco music hits.

PHOTOGRAPHS AND VIDEOS – The way to preserve a precious event such as this is to make sure that every moment is captured through photographs and videos.

I still have my photo album, which I flip through once in a while. I don't have a video that I can play over and over, but the photos are enough to remind me of all the special people who shared this momentous occasion with me. I still crack up when I see myself in that Thumbelina gown, smile when I remember all the friends and classmates who had a great time, especially the ones who later ended up marrying

163

their dates, and get teary eyed when I see those of the friends and relatives who have passed.

Currently, the Philippine debut is still a much-anticipated event in Filipino culture. A few rituals or original ideas have been added, but the true meaning stays the same. Other than it primarily being a Filipina's rite of passage to adulthood, it is a celebration held with family and those dear to the debutante.

If my father were still here today, I would thank him profusely for his way of showing me how much he loved me. When I was celebrating mine, my vision was clouded because of my childish expectations. I kept moping because I didn't have a mother, a suitor or a boyfriend on my 18th birthday. I also used to look back at it as a debut not as spectacular as all the other debuts I attended after mine, but later in life, I see my father as a loving father who did his best. And that is all that should have mattered. Each time I reminisce on my debut, I recall each moment with fond memories and gratitude.

A Filipino-American resident of North Highlands, CA, Christine "Chrissi" L. Villa is the founder of Purple Cotton Candy Arts, a fast-growing business that offers publishing services to children's authors. She has written 10 children's books since 2014, three of which won awards in the Northern California Publishers and Authors Book Award Competitions of 2018, 2019, and 2020. Two of these titles are now available in bilingual editions (English/Filipino) and one of these titles is available in bilingual editions (English/Filipino and English/Spanish).

Next to writing children's books, she is passionate about writing short-form poems such as haiku, tanka, and cherita. Her poems have appeared in numerous online and print journals worldwide. She has garnered several awards and has published her first poetry book entitled The Bluebird's Cry.

She is the founding editor of Frameless Sky, the first haiku and tanka journal available in DVD, and of Velvet Dusk Publishing.

If she is not writing or publishing, she dabbles in alcohol ink painting, doodling, mixed media, and photography.

You can learn more about Chrissi at www.christinevilla.com.

A DICKENS' REVIEW

SUSAN BETH FURST

"Charles Dickens' great-great-grandson?"

She peered over the top of her horn-rimmed glasses, nodded her head, and whispered, "Yes, he will be performing *A Christmas Carol* at the Ebenezer Baptist Church at precisely two o'clock."

I grabbed the last ticket and pointed my wheelie toward the front of the store. I had exactly one hour to eat lunch and get up that hill to the church.

"Don't be late," she called after me. "Once the performance begins, the doors will be closed, tight as a drum!"

The church was small. I sat in the back pew by the window. Gerald Charles Dickens looked every bit the handsome young Scrooge as he walked to the front of the church and turned to face the audience.

"Marley was dead…

as a doornail."

The gravity of the moment was punctuated, ever so briefly, by an inconvenient car alarm. Dickens mentioned crickets.

Scrooge and Marley conversed as Dickens hopped back and forth, to the right of the coat rack and then to the left, then the left and back to the right. The voices were distinct, but Dickens remained the same. At the end of the scene, Dickens followed an invisible Jacob Marley to the back of the church, where Marley flew out of the window to a life of never-ending torment.

Dickens was four feet from me. I resisted the temptation to touch him.

"Bah Humbug!"

Dickens was Scrooge, and Marley and the ghosts of Christmas Past, Present, and Future. He was the incorrigible Topper, Scrooge's nephew and his wife, and his wife's sister. He was Tiny Tim, and all the little Cratchits at once. But when it came to Mrs. Cratchit, queen of the plum pudding and plunger of the carving knife, no one could hold a candle to him. And the gush of stuffing from the goose, well, Dickens had that down too, like chestnuts roasting.

"And so, as Tiny Tim observed, God Bless Us, Every One!"

Dickens' performance was met with hearty applause. My fellow travelers and I rushed out to meet him. I handed him a copy of my new book hastily procured from my car, wrapped in leftover tissue paper, and topped with a stray Christmas Cracker.

"Thank you!" he said graciously, in his authentic Dickensian kind of way.

It was later when I read his blog that I found a photo of my book, still wrapped in tissue paper, the Cracker slightly askew. And there was a comment: *"a charming children's Christmas Book."*

I noticed the alliteration. Dickens' genes, I thought. And then I smiled. I'd snagged a review from the great-great-grandson of Charles Dickens. Never mind that he didn't mention the title or the author. I knew, and that was enough. After all, the proof is in the pudding!

A CHRISTMAS OF CONSEQUENCES

DANIEL SCHMITT

N o season is quite like Christmas for welling up memories, and no Christmas season incident is more indelibly seared into my memory than the one that occurred on Christmas Day 1960.

But for you to grasp the significance of that happening, you must first be introduced to the Schmitt family.

I grew up the third of seven children in the small north-central Wisconsin town of Schofield. Six of the seven Schmitt kids were boys, and we were all-boy, if you know what I mean.

Perhaps more appropriately, looking back through the lens of some 60 years, a neighborhood spinster, a real curmudgeon who had absolutely zero appreciation for any male under the age of twenty, pegged it accurately when she referred to us as those "feral Schmitt kids."

There was never a dearth of misdeeds, ill behavior, and outright stupidity on the part of us boys. Whether it involved getting caught stealing one of Mrs. Fox's home-grown watermelons, or coming home with a bloody nose caused by a fist fight with a neighbor lad, my parents, products of the Great Depression and World War II, disciplined us differently. Mom's disciplinary modus operandi was to shame and pain us boys into righteousness by first sobbing and uttering loudly, "Where did we go wrong?" We boys always assumed that by "we", Mom meant her and Dad, not us, but that was of little consolation because her next move was to bring out the paddle.

Dad, on the other hand, didn't really have a method of discipline; it was more a philosophy of life. I never heard my dad swear or saw him get angry. I guess after living through the Great Depression, landing on Omaha Beach D-Day plus four, and fighting the Germans in the Battle of the Bulge, raising six boys was a piece of cake. So, whatever the wrong-doing, Mother would get hysterical while Dad would calmly say, "Well, it happened before; I'm sure it'll happen again." That was it. We never took Dad's "I'm sure it'll happen again" as license to repeat the transgression. Dad had a way with words.

Those words were put to the test that Christmas of my twelfth year. Growing up in a Catholic family, Christmas was supposed to be about Baby Jesus' birth and how he had come down to earth to save us.

Truth be told, no Schmitt boy put much stock in that story. We just couldn't wrap our little pea brains around it, and we most assuredly never entertained the idea that we needed saving. We viewed the Christmas season as a once-a-year wonderful holiday of tree trimming and feasting on shrimp, pickled herring, Mom's special cheese dips and all sorts of homemade Christmas cookies.

Mostly, Christmas was about getting presents, and that Christmas, Santa had brought me a Daisy Pellet Rifle, the best present ever!

The ecstasy of graduating from the BB gun to a pellet rifle couldn't be contained, and immediately after Christmas morning breakfast, my older brother Rick and I headed out into a freezing, snowy blizzard for a couple of hours of "shooting" in the woods just behind the old Hoffmeister's Grocery Store.

When I think back upon the incident now, I wonder if it was the blizzard conditions that caused things to go so terribly wrong. You see, brother Rick, even at the age of fourteen, was considered the best young marksman in the neighborhood.

Well, as we approached the grocery store, we decided to shoot at the gas pump directly in front of the huge storefront window. Rick shot first, and his first shot was the last. To this day, he claims we were 50 yards away from the pump. I believe it was no more than 20 feet. Whatever the distance, he took aim, pulled the trigger, missed the pump and the pellet went smack dab through the store window!

Knowing we'd be in big trouble if caught, we did what any boys in that situation would have done – we turned and sprinted for home, two blocks away. Unfortunately for us, a neighbor lady was looking out her front window, saw everything and promptly called our parents.

Hustling up the hill to our house, the best young marksman in the neighborhood decided we should use the family car's back license plate for target practice. Sounded great to me! Rick aimed, pulled the trigger, and "PLING," we heard the sound of the pellet hit its target.

Then, it was my turn. I cocked the rifle, steadied my body, fixed the sights on the license plate and pulled the trigger. The sound we were expecting did not come. Rather it was more like a THUD, and we watched in horror as the back car window honeycombed and shattered into hundreds of tiny pieces. Missed again!

Entering the kitchen through the back door, we immediately realized we were in deep doodoo! Mom was crying uncontrollably but still managed to get out in sporadic bursts, "Where...did...we...go...wrong?"

Dad chimed in with "Well, it happened before; I'm sure it'll happen again." But then he added, "You boys will have to pay for that store window."

Rick and I looked at each other and our eyes said it all, "Phew, they don't know about the car window!"

That changed the next morning. Rick and I slept in the same bedroom. We didn't get much sleep that night because we knew what was coming. We heard the back door slam shut, a sign that Dad was heading off to work. A few minutes later, we again heard the door slam. Dad came into our bedroom, turned the light on and calmly said, "Now you boys got a store window and a car window to pay for." And then, uncharacteristically, he added, "Oh, and the pellet gun is mine until both windows are paid for."

Brother Rick had a paper route and was making decent money for a kid his age, about $10 per week. He paid off his share of the windows in no time. I, on the other hand, shoveled lots of neighborhood driveways that winter. The going rate back then was about 50 cents per job, so it wasn't until mid-spring that I got my pellet rifle back.

I swear on a holy manger no future Christmas brought one-tenth the discomfort to my parents as did that Christmas of my twelfth year. I had that gun until I left home for the military at the age of eighteen, and I will also swear that it was never again used to shoot windows.

Daniel Schmitt is a retired English and social science teacher, and has been dabbling with writing for the better part of forty years.

Usually, he writes short pieces, and gets inspirations from personal experiences like travelling, hiking, and simply observing the world and people around him. He especially enjoys recounting some of the youthful experiences he had growing up in north-central Wisconsin. Writing, like reading, constantly opens his mind to new experiences and ways of thinking, and brings him lots of enjoyment.

THANKSGIVING MEANS TURKEY, NOT SHRIMP

NORMA JEAN THORNTON

Growing up in a resort area with self-employed parents who owned a garage, gas station and emergency towing service which required being available 365 days a year, 24/7, and their busiest times were holidays, we didn't take vacations, go places, or heavily celebrate holidays like an average family, but we did celebrate Thanksgiving and Christmas, at least a little.

Mostly Thanksgiving, because our folks would completely close the station, and for years, we went out of town for a day or two, over 100 miles from home, to "The Tent" where Mom cooked the turkey while Daddy hunted pheasant.

For Christmas, Daddy would open the station after the presents were unwrapped, and close up at dinner-time.

Every year, Daddy always bought each of "his girls" - Mom, my two younger sisters and me - a heart-shaped box of candy on Valentine's Day, took each of us shopping for a new outfit, and/or a new pair of shoes sometime around Easter, and gave us kids money to buy fireworks for the 4th of July…and he BBQ'd.

Mom always handled costumes for Halloween; Easter stuff, cooking for Thanksgiving, Christmas, and everything else. But Mom didn't BBQ.

Led by me, the girls and I took care of Mother's Day and Father's Day, which normally consisted of three homemade cards for each, and some small present…one year we replaced the pancake turner Mom had broken earlier when she spanked one of my younger sisters.

Mom happily showed us how much she appreciated it,

by using it immediately on all three of us, for being such smart-asses. I learned quickly she was obviously smarter than we were! I wonder if I'd not written the snarky note in the card that the pancake turner was to replace the one she'd broken on XXX, if Mom wouldn't have known that's why we got it for her? Nah. She'd have known anyway. Moms always know those things.

Then there was the anniversary cake we tried to make for Mom and Daddy, that wound up dubbed the "Earthquake Cake"; we found out what happens when stacking three round cake layers before letting them cool, then trying to cover up the goof by filling-in those cracks with a whole bunch of extra, sweet white powdered sugar frosting. Since it was close to Valentine's Day, we topped it with a bunch of red-hot candies, with the majority in a pile in the middle, trying to cover up that huge crack!

One saving grace...it was really moist, and tasted great!

There were times growing up, when holidays weren't celebrated on the actual day, and my high school graduation was cut short because Daddy got a call as we were leaving. We all went in the same car, and as soon as the ceremony was over, we all went home because Daddy had that tow job, plus it was a resort town and Memorial Day weekend, when all the crazies were out, creating lots of wrecks.

But I digress, so back to Mom's major holiday contributions.

To us girls, Christmas was mostly about presents, Thanksgiving was the food: "stuffed turkey and all the fixin's": mashed potatoes and gravy, candied sweet potatoes, homemade yeast rolls and a veggie...plus pumpkin, apple, berry and custard pies, with coconut cake for Daddy.

For Christmas, it was the special sweet stuff: homemade cookies we all helped bake (Daddy sampled), plus Mom's award-winning, raved-about homemade candy she started working on the day after Thanksgiving, which was immediately after we got home from our pheasant hunting trip to "The Tent".

Thanksgiving was the only time the station was closed, and we "got away from it all" to celebrate as a family, so possibly it's the distinct things from Thanksgiving that cause all those memories to return each time I have turkey.

November 1941 to 1946:

My Thanksgiving remembrances before I was six are a blur, because we traveled a lot during the holidays back and forth between Sacramento and Missouri where my folks were born, prior to moving from Sacramento to Clearlake in July of 1947. Then, until I was almost eleven, we had Thanksgiving every year with Daddy's family, especially the young cousins, on their property where we hunted, somewhere in Northern California, with kids playing and the adults pheasant hunting.

My two younger sisters were born 16 months apart when I was 8 and 10. Shortly after the youngest was born, Daddy's cousins, whose property we had hunted, moved to Washington State, so Daddy joined a hunting association in Sutter County,120 miles from home, and we traveled daily to just north of Sacramento to continue pheasant hunting for the duration.

Daddy soon made friends with a local property owner, and the following year, our Thanksgivings continued from the inside of a HUGE United States Army chow-tent our parents bought and left set up on that property for almost the entire pheasant season – a whole month – each year, until around 1966.

November 1947:

The first year after we moved from Sacramento, two full months of excitement, surrounded by pheasant hunting, and cousins, started the first week of November every year during opening day of pheasant season. The wonderful smells of fried pheasant and all the holiday foods, enhanced by pies the week of Thanksgiving, continued into December, with Mom's baking and candy-making through Christmas.

My everlasting memory as a child: Mom would be in the kitchen once again getting ready for Christmas, making her special sweet traditions…fudges and divinity candies…and Daddy's favorite, Ice Box Cookies! (AKA Refrigerator

Cookies)

(Thus, my passion for writing and publishing rustic cookbooks: especially candies and baked sweets that led to soups, then a variety of cookbooks, all with good-old fashioned-down-home cooking).

November 1952:

Daddy would drag out the humongous WWII military cook-tent and they'd set it up in that huge field a few miles north of Rio Linda. (It was strictly by coincidence that ten years later, I wound up living in Rio Linda, not eight miles from the Thanksgiving location of "The Tent".)

Cots and sleeping bags were arranged around the inside perimeter of one section of "The Tent", with ice-chests, tables, a huge cook-stove and oven, and anything else to do with a kitchen, placed together in another section. An enormous pot-bellied heating stove, situated in the very center, helped warm the entire 20' x 48' huge-room-sized tent.

Many of our families and friends, hunters or not, came from all around to visit, have a bite to eat, hunt, or spend a night or longer at "The Tent".

Late Thanksgiving Eve, Mom would make the dressing and stuff the turkey at home, then wrap it all in foil and put it on ice for the less than two-hour drive Thanksgiving Day, so it could immediately be popped into the huge oven in "The Tent" to be ready for dinner once the day's hunt was over.

There was always someone at "The Tent" from the day it was set up until the day it was torn down the Sunday after Thanksgiving.

After Thanksgiving, with all that delectable pie and turkey-left-over-goodness polished off, we were back home, our visual senses overwhelmed for a month, by dark brown chocolate fudge, the golden brown of peanut butter fudge, and white, green and pink divinity, many in fluffy candy-kiss shapes, some with nuts.

There were also milk chocolate fudge squares, peanut butter fudge squares, and pink, green and white coconut fudge squares. Some had nuts, some didn't.

The pink and green holiday colors may have excited

our visual senses and the delightful aromas of warm chocolate, peanut butter, and coconut overloaded our olfactory senses, but waking up each morning, for days, to the tantalizing smells was heavenly, and the sampling that we always got, was like something out of a fairy tale, leaving wonderful memories for more than 75 years thus far.

November 1958:

After graduating, I stayed with cousins in Sacramento while in college, so instead of going "home" for Thanksgiving, we'd drive the 15 miles or so to "The Tent" for that weekend each year. I married, had two kids, and moved to Rio Linda in December 1962.

November 1963:

That year, and the following plus a couple more before the land-owner died and Daddy lost the land-use for "The Tent", I made cornbread and wild-rice dressing, stuffed and roasted the Thanksgiving turkey in Mom's roaster at my home, made the gravy, then took it to "The Tent", where Mom and my younger sisters had pies and everything else ready.

After that, for a few years my parents went from pheasant hunting to taking my younger sisters fishing in Florida a couple of weeks each year, so I took over total hosting of the Thanksgiving Feast. My parents always made it a point to be back home from their Florida fishing trips in time to join the gradually growing group of attendees.

Over those years, I eventually added appetizers and snacks, plus a bunch of wild game meats from Hubby and the kids' hunts (venison and antelope roast, sometimes pheasant), and a plethora of other specially requested goodies from Hubby and a couple of grands, in addition to the rest of the usual Thanksgiving fare, but no matter how many other meats I may have included, turkey is what makes it Thanksgiving to me, and except for only one Thanksgiving in my so-far 80 years, that's exactly what I've always had.

November 1978:

Hubby had an early morning appointment with a doctor in San Francisco the day before Thanksgiving, and, reminiscent of my childhood while being flexible on most holidays, we celebrated our normal...although early...full turkey dinner with all the family the Sunday before the traditional turkey-day, allowing the kids to be with their significant others, or cousins, to celebrate *the* "T" Day, and Hubby and I left Tuesday in the motorhome, with holiday leftovers in the fridge, headed to San Francisco.

We found a parking lot that accepted RVs under the Bay Bridge, not far from the doctor, and spent the night, got up, went to the doctor, then headed down the coast on Hwy 1, for parts unknown, for the weekend.

After what felt like *hours*, we realized finding an RV park or any type campground at that time of year was next to impossible so we pulled into a rest stop for a quick rest because I was about to fall asleep...and I was driving.

We were aware of the increasing criminal violence against travelers during that time, with vehicles being broken into, and travelers sometimes beaten, or worse, at California rest stops, but it was either take a chance on that, or fall asleep at the wheel. My husband was a police officer, authorized to always carry his gun in the entire state of California, so we felt fairly safe with that extra bit of security.

Unfortunately, we quickly found rest stops still might not be a good idea, when a knock on the door surprised both my husband, and the CHP officer who was at the door, when hubby answered it with a pistol in one hand. After the initial shock and explanations on both parts, the officer advised us that "camping" there, no matter for how long, was a no-no, and with a slight smirk, and cryptic directions, told us how to get to the nearest campground, a few miles down the road.

We found the worn RV sign just after dusk, and turned off highway 1 onto a bumpy, sandy, pot-hole-filled dirt "path" – definitely not a road – that would make do-it-yourself off-road 4-wheel drive and jeep trails in the mountains seem like super-highways. Some of the potholes and ruts were so deep I wasn't sure we were going to make it in...and even more worried about once in, would we ever be able to make it back out!? Even though the sign indicated there was RV space, we were glad ours wasn't any bigger than 28'.

There were many hand-painted and written signs all around, but hard to read in the full darkness that had fallen by the time we slowly made it through that dusty maze, to the gates of entry at the well-hidden, off-the-beaten-path RV/campground.

Surprisingly, it was a popular place: there were four motorhomes of varying sizes waiting ahead of us at the closed gate, with a separate line for customers to stand at the booth to pay. Hubby went to get in line, and the guy in the big rig ahead of us walked by carrying a long, slinky cat. I opened the window and asked about the cat, since we also had cats, and stated I was amazed they had made it, with their larger rig, and the driving conditions, getting into the place. He shared that they had been going there for years. More odd conversation, about hoping it was a good experience for us, since it was our first time, and he was sure we'd be back. Shades of *Alice in Wonderland*...things were getting "curiouser and curiouser"!

Only two spaces away from the outhouse restrooms and garbage cans, we found our spot, a slab of concrete in a row of about 20 concrete slabs, right next to the big rig that had been ahead of us. The slabs were only about 3' apart, with no hookups, which meant once parked, we were set, and went straight to bed, too tired to even fight getting out in the damp and drizzly, to dump our small sack of garbage.

With the dawn, there was no more curiosity...things became *quite clear*, thanks to our new next-door neighbor, who had been carrying the cat the night before and I had spoken with.

First thing that morning, I put on sweats and a jacket, because it was cold and dreary out, grabbed the garbage, and headed to the garbage cans at the outhouse slab. It was windy, my head was down as I walked, and I literally bumped right into our neighbor, who was coming out of the restrooms just as I started to dump the trash...he was buck-naked from the waist down, except for his shoes (yes, the cold had an extreme effect on him), but he **was** wearing a jacket.

I was mortified, red-faced, stuttered an apology, almost

dropped the garbage, and forced myself to not follow the urge to run as fast as I could back to our motorhome, where I yelled at my husband to "...get out of bed and get your clothes on; we're getting the hell out of here!"

Obviously, we were at a nudist, clothes optional beach-campground, and that damned CHP officer conveniently failed to clearly tell us that. We finally made it back onto Hwy 1 and found a campground somewhere in Santa Cruz, where we heated leftover Thanksgiving dinner in the microwave. It tasted as good as it first did the Sunday before, with all the family.

November 1987:

As usual, our house was filled with family, friends, neighbors and coworkers, so Thanksgiving was the normal hectic, with *"Too many helpers trying to get in the kitchen, ready to 'spill' the broth."*

Partially pulling out the oven rack and removing the foil from the turkey for one last baste, the very-helpful overly-anxious youngest married son filled the baster too full. It spit and splattered grease and other good gravy-making turkey-juices on the oven door, the floor, him and even in the oven. Instead of wiping it up, he shoved the turkey back in to let it finish cooking, the spilled grease wound up 'cooked' on the door, and the bottom of the oven, plus smoking a bit, making an oven-cleaning necessary.

This was a fairly-new, self-cleaning oven, one which I had never had the need to use that great perk for before, so was unfamiliar with the directions...except what it said on the magic knob, about how to turn it on to clean. Piece of cake, right? WRONG! Rather than wipe up the small amount of grease left in the oven, after dinner, it was decided that magic oven would just automatically clean anything, so the magic cleaning knob was turned.

If you have one of those ovens, I'm here to tell you, you'd best wipe up any grease lurking in the bottom before letting the auto-clean take over, or all hell will break loose. At least it did with us: cleaning temperature is between 700°-900° but the door also automatically locks and won't unlock, no matter what, until it cools down to a normal oven-usage temp.

In addition, that very hot temperature caught the spilled grease on fire, making inside the oven explode like a roaring fireplace, and we were forced to call the fire department, to the chagrin of my husband and all four of our fully grown adult sons who were totally incapable of getting the door open.

When the six muscular firemen couldn't open it either, my five also-muscular 'boys' were relieved they hadn't lost their man-cards. HOWEVER, we had to wait several hours for the fire to burn out, at the expense of the two rear burners, with burned-out wires, and partially melted plastic knobs on the front of the stove...that stupid "magic" one, included.

November 1990:

The first year we took the motorhome instead of flying to our annual white-tail deer hunt in Missouri, Hubby wanted Thanksgiving in Tombstone, Arizona, because he had been stationed at Fort Huachuca many years before. I was looking forward to turkey, but it was late when we got there, and there was just one restaurant open. I wound up with shrimp because the last turkey dinner was ordered by the people who beat us in the door. I bitched about it for years – and still do! *Thanksgiving Means Turkey, not Shrimp!*

November 2002:

In the motorhome again, on our way home from another of our annual Missouri White-Tail Hunts, we stopped for an early Thanksgiving dinner at the *Golden Corral* in Norman, Oklahoma, then on to San Antonio, Texas to visit my widowed baby-sister who was camp host in an RV park. We parked next to her, and I baked a really quick chicken stuffed with a mix of boxed wild-rice and packaged cornbread dressing, with all the usual extras, as a second Thanksgiving for the three of us. Dinner was ready by the time she got off work, and we ate outside her motor home on her picnic table.

November 2003:

Hawaii! We had a plated Thanksgiving dinner at Honolulu's famous Pink Lady – the *Royal Hawaiian* - and it was *horrible,* as well as the most expensive turkey-day meal we ever had. The bird was seasoned with garlic and undercooked, the plain bread dressing was wet and gooey, and the mashed potatoes were filled with garlic *and* potato peels - I hate both, but especially garlic. Even the pie was the worst - not only wet and undercooked, but sweet potato instead of pumpkin. Needless to say, we went back to our hotel across the street (Sheraton Princess Kaiulani - the PK) hungry, and wound-up ordering pizza from around the corner.

We should have eaten the Thanksgiving Buffet at the PK.

November 2005:
Our last Thanksgiving together I was staying at the hospital with my husband, so our eldest daughter-in-law did Thanksgiving. After their late afternoon dinner, she and our son brought a plate of turkey and all the fixin's for each of us. I ate all the turkey from both our plates.

November 2006 to 2019:
My parents and husband passed, then two granddaughters and my sister; neighbors and friends have retired or moved. Our brood of kids, grands and greats has slowly dwindled to only five still living in California, and after cooking for between 30-50 almost every Thanksgiving, I can't adjust to cooking for so few, so Thanksgiving dinner has been taken over by my oldest daughter...who cooks duck and ham because she doesn't like turkey. Duck's fine, but it's not turkey, so I happily split my Thanksgiving dinner and lunch, between her house and the *Golden Corral*, in order to have my turkey!

Actually, with the exception of wild game, eating at the *Golden Corral* every day is like eating at my house at Thanksgiving, because what we had was always more like a buffet with the stuff I fixed special for each of the kids and hubby... cornbread and beans, mac'n'cheese, potato salad, green salad and all the toppings for those dieting or vegan, a variety of regular, plus game meats (cooked a variety of ways), and cheeses in addition to the roast turkey, mashed potatoes and gravy, cornbread and wild rice dressing, candied sweet potatoes, a variety of chips and dips (bean, guacamole, ranch, artichoke/parmesan), salsa, shrimp cocktail, an antipasto tray filled with veggies and other munchies, plus homemade candy, pies…and ham.

November 2020:

Thanks to the COVID pandemic, *Golden Corral* wasn't open, but at lunchtime, my neighbors brought over a plate of turkey and fixin's, totally different than ours, but still good; the local granddaughter also roasted a turkey and delivered me a plate of all her good stuff for dinner, so I got my double dose of turkey, and there's still only the one year I didn't have any of that delectable bird!

Once she's ready for it full-time, the Thanksgiving tradition will soon be bestowed upon the oldest daughter's youngest daughter who's the only grand still living in our area…fortunately, she loves turkey.

November 2021:

In the meantime, *Golden Corral*, here I come!

Her baby sister called her Nonie, her great-granddaughter calls her GumGum.

Norma Jean Thornton, AKA Noniedoodles, a multiple County and State Fair award-winning baker, candy-maker, art-doodler, plus award-winning writing granny from Rio Linda, California, creates her doodle-art and dabbles with her writings at the computer, with unwanted help from her feisty cats.

lulu.com/spotlight/nonie
lulu.com/spotlight/TheGrannysWritings
normathornton@yahoo.com

*"Love Never Dies" in Harlequin's Inspirational Anthology, A Kiss Under the Mistletoe
*Nonie's Big Bottom Girls' Rio Linda Cookbooks (4)
*Nonie's "Stuff" Cookbooks (Candy &...Stuff; Cookies...&...Stuff; Soups &...Stuff)
*Nosie Rosie's Diaries: (True cat diaries, written by The Granny & The Windy--Years 1 & 2 of 16-years)
*Nonie's Cat Anthologies (Fun, not-so-fun, sometimes crazy short cat stories) 2 Volumes
*Nonie's Wet Kitty Kisses Anthologies (Mostly humorous Shorts) 2 Volumes
*noniedoodles coloring books (artwork by Nonie's original doodles) Several Volumes
*Doodles the Dorky Dragon, in the Dorky Land of Noniedoodles

*Every 2019, 2020 & 2021 NCPA Anthology

HOLIDAZE...FROM A CAT'S VIEW
KNIGHTLY NACHT, THE CAT &
ROBERTA "BERT" DAVIS

C at Journal: These are the holiday experiences by your host, Nacht, the house panther:
Boy, I'm glad we're still in England. There's my human over there, watching fireworks on the big screen. Fourth of July, it's called. Here in England, it's more like, "Good riddance, peasants!"

I remember back home in the states. Humans would blow up crap all week. These were the same humans who would yell at me for yowling at night, and it wasn't even me yowling! The lady cats were making most of the noise: "Nacht, I'm so lonely! Step into my parlor!"

* * *

Nacht curled up beside Celeste, who was still watching fireworks. She had mentioned going back to the states, but sometimes she would mention leaving the planet. People often thought she said crazy things, but crazy or not, if she said something, it usually happened. Nacht decided he appreciated fireworks this way, with the volume turned down, and music in the background.

As he drifted off to sleep, the memories swirled into hazy dreams.

* * *

It was the third night of his neighborhood in the States, sounding like a war zone. His block, of all places! There were more dogs than usual on the streets. At least most of them were more interested in hiding than chasing cats. Still, some chased cats, squirrels, and any other smaller prey.

Even without seeing any loose dogs nearby, none of the animals needed chasing to run about in a craze. Nacht witnessed mama birds fleeing their nests, and ground-wildlife rushing about in chaos.

One mother squirrel left her kids, her shiny eyes full of fear. She fled past Nacht's hiding spot in the bushes. Not looking back, the squirrel charged up a tall pole.

"Hey," Nacht said, peeking out of his safe spot. "What about your kids?"

He received no reply except unintelligible chittering. The baby squirrels tried following her, their eyes barely open, not up for such a climb. As Nacht went to the pole to yell at the mother, the baby squirrels gathered around him, snuggling and clawing at his fur.

"Ow! Wait, not me. Quit it!"

The young ones didn't relent, all three of them, seeking comfort from him. One tried to nurse, shoving at Nacht's belly with the persistence of a baby goat demanding milk.

"Ow! Oh, no you don't," Nacht refused, squirming away. He glowered far up the pole, but couldn't see the mother. "Get back here," he yowled, "now!"

More fireworks lit up the sky, slicing through the darkness with angry shards of colors.

Nacht retreated to his bushes with the baby squirrels close in tow. He curled up again, now with his unexpected foster kids. The cat heaved a sigh. "Drafted as a nursemaid for baby nut-hunters," he fumed. "I hope the other cats don't find out."

He waited all night for the mother to return. May as well, for he had a good spot and for some unknown reason felt protective over the babies. Nacht was exhausted, hungry, thirsty, and as outright cranky as a cat in a bath. It was too hot to sleep by day and too noisy at night. The whole event made him wonder why he wanted outside in the first place. He didn't even know why his old humans let him outside.

Nacht was one of only a few animals savvy enough to stay in his hiding spot. How could humans call shrieking, fiery skies fun? Were they truly having a good time? They must be enjoying all the hoopla. He heard music and whoops of excited humans, engines, and all kinds of clamor.

He waited hours that felt like days for the commotion to stop. After clobbering his belly for quite some time, the baby squirrels settled down more from weariness than his annoyed grumbles and hissing. Somebody was cooking meat nearby, and didn't even invite him. Rude, rotten rats! He was too upset to eat anyway, a rare mood for Nacht.

By some miracle, the mother squirrel did approach, in the wee hours of the morning. She shyly investigated the area, then hesitated at the sight of the black cat surrounded by her young.

Nacht flicked his ears sideways in clear annoyance. "You left them with me. Take them, slacker."

Nacht used his nose to push the babies toward her, and then sprinted away, glad to escape the brats again. They had scratched him, tried to nurse, leaving wet spots on his belly, a bad image indeed for a tom cat. But in their innocence, they appreciated him. Stupid fireworks caused by ridiculous humans!

*   *   *

A ringing noise lulled him out of dreamland, along with soft petting. He woke beside Celeste, who was adoringly settling him farther back on the chair.

"Don't roll off," she said with a smile, and moved off to answer her phone.

Whew, was he glad to be back in the waking world with her. Nacht seemed to end up with traveling people, but so far, Celeste was the best.

Maybe he could appreciate holidays now. Most holidays seemed to orbit around humans getting in the sack, or drunk, or both.

Nacht held New Year's Day with almost as much disdain as that week in July, with enough noise and stupor that could drive animals to drink. Then came Valentine's Day, ugh! "I'm glad we cats don't have to buy chocolates; can't eat the stuff anyway."

On St. Patrick's Day, humans got drunk. They did this

on most holidays. There are various Dead Guy Days, which is really weird. Easter, where humans think rabbits make-out with chickens. Gross! The infamous Fourth of July. He hissed inwardly and tried to repress memories of long nights with fireworks, gunshots, sirens, and the paranoia it caused among animals.

What could cheer him up? Ah, Halloween, a controversial night for cats. It was amusing, though. Humans lost all sense of identity on the night they dressed up in fantastical costumes. Maybe Celeste would make him a knight costume and let him hunt for fresh vermin. Yum.

Thanksgiving was his favorite. Even with lame humans, he found exquisite treats. Who could turn down turkey and stuffing? On the downside, human food often made him sick, or it used to. Even his queasy stomach was fading into memories. His new chef brought treats, yummy cat food, and un-spiced meat for him to eat.

As for Christmas, living with Celeste had made Christmas feel like it was year-round.

Nacht had experienced holidays in Europe as well. The Maypole… humans partied around that thing like rabbits in heat. The same humans had the nerve to shoo him away when he started climbing up the ribbons. Bah! If a cat can't climb it, what's it good for?

On Swan Upping Day, Europeans caught and released swans, and let them swim down the River Thames. The birds flouted their beauty and grace while posing as an escaping buffet that nobody could eat. To a cat, they looked like oversized toys amidst a floating buffet.

Brewfests weren't bad. Saucy humans shared food more than usual, especially big, yummy brats.

For now, Nacht felt like he had it made. His new human hadn't thrown one big party. She protected him like a cat guarding a new toy, and she doted over him instead of other humans.

Nacht fell back to sleep, dreaming of the best holiday on the planet, National Cat Day.

* * *

Knightly Nacht, a fairly young savvy, black cat, has been tame, then semi feral, and "tame" again. His past street time and traveling owners helped him evolve into a brave, gentlemanly pirate of felines. He nabs food when he must but would rather schmooze the ladies.

A complex sort, Nacht tells stories to other animals and thusly, narrates the stories using his name in a manner that humans can understand. He has a close bond with his human Celeste, who happens to understand cat language. He is like a modern guardian familiar to her.

Nacht's story unfolds a bit with each anthology tale, and his purrsonality is a compilation of some of Berta's cats and a few strays she's re-tamed, fostered, and adopted out. Rumor has it that Nacht and Celeste's bloodlines may not be entirely from Earth, but that is another story.

Roberta "Bert" Davis, pen name "Berta D," is a life-long writer of Science-Fiction, Fantasy, and Techno Thrillers. She's currently the lead technical writer and graphic design artist for equipment manuals and has written sci-fi since childhood.

Bert has spent much of her life in animal groups, working with cat rescue. She has spent nearly ten years learning about cat needs and their behavior, both tame and untamed. She is working on a series starring cats and a few human helpers. Roberta has done TNR or rescue for years, and has helped over a dozen cats get indoor homes. She maintains a small colony of feral cats who came with the current home. Wild ex-wild kitties are a big influence in her short stories. She has four ex-feral pet cats inside, named Raggle Taggle, Luna Lovepaw, Mr. Tibbles, and Hufflepoof "Poofy."

Roberta is published in multiple anthologies, two from SSWC, and several cat stories in NCPA anthologies. Her sci-fi novel, more of a life's work, is in the process of being published.

THE CHRISTMAS SPIRIT

SANDRA D. SIMMER

C hristmas was much less commercialized when I was a child. In my small rural community in Southwest Colorado, I remember it as magical in its simplicity. There weren't multiple holiday festivals to attend, or massive light displays, or televised Christmas specials clamoring for our attention for weeks. Christmas decorations were only put out for sale in the stores after Thanksgiving. The season was focused on the birth of Christ through unadorned church gatherings, and extended family celebrations. There was only one exception.

The local K-8 elementary school would put on an elaborate Christmas pageant every year. It was the highlight of the holiday season and the entire community would attend. Every student in the school had some part in the production. Children might sing in the chorus, perform a solo, or say a few lines in the play, but everyone had their role to perform. We would practice songs and rehearse our parts all fall in preparation for the big production.

I started first grade in 1961 in the same four-room schoolhouse my parents had attended in the 1930's. My teacher, Mrs. Holder, taught the first three grades in the big room at the east end of the building. Mrs. Porter, (one of my mother's cousins), had the middle room, and taught fourth and fifth grade. On the other side of the hall, there was one long room extending the length of the building. It could be divided by large wooden folding panels. Mrs. Campbell taught sixth and seventh grade in half of the big room. The other half of the big room contained a stage and a piano at the far end. It was also the classroom for the eighth-grade students taught by the principal, Mrs. Koskie, (a longtime friend of my mother).

We would practice our songs and rehearse our parts with our classroom teacher all week, and then on Fridays everyone would go into "the big kids' classroom" to sing around the piano. The multi-talented Mrs. Koskie would play the piano while we practiced our Christmas songs. We belted out our renditions of *Joy to the World* and *O Little Town of Bethlehem*. In our secluded part of the world, *O Come, All Ye Faithful* applied to all in attendance.

The Christmas play of 1961 was my first time to participate, and the one I remember the best. The other years blend into a blur of seasonal carols and forgettable skits. But that year, Mrs. Koskie and the other teachers made a brave move. They chose to put on a play titled *Santa Claus in Outer Space*. Whether the ladies wrote it themselves or purchased a copy, it was quite the adventurous undertaking for our back-country school. In May that year, President Kennedy had announced to Congress the goal of sending a man to the moon by end of the decade. The whole country was caught up in the idea of man venturing beyond Earth's atmosphere. Our little school took part in the excitement by producing a space related Christmas play.

Students were given roles as aliens from all the planets in our solar system. I was one of the three girls, in the first-grade class of seven students, assigned to represent the planet, Venus. Our sparkly blue costumes reflected light when we walked on stage to say one line in unison; "We are visitors from the planet Venus." One of the older boys gave a whistle, as we were supposed to be beautiful Venusian maidens. It was very exciting! All the planetary representatives in the play came together at one gathering place to solve their disagreements. Everyone was at odds competing for recognition and power until Santa Claus arrived as the representative from Earth. He was able to bring peace to the group by teaching them about the Spirit of Christmas.

The Saturday night of the big event, my mother, father, and even my teenage sister, came to watch my acting debut. The double doors of the big room were pulled open to make one large room facing the stage. Fathers came to the school early in the day to stack all the desks in the middle room. They set up rows of folding chairs hauled from the Grange Hall to make a theater at the school. By curtain time, every seat was full and there was standing room only in the back. The excitement of the cast and audience alike filled the air with anticipation.

The evening's production was a huge success. All the students remembered their lines, the Christmas carols were joyous, and the audience joined in at the end to sing a rousing rendition of *Hark the Herald Angels Sing*. It seemed as if everyone greatly enjoyed the evening. However, we did go back to more traditional themes after that year. Maybe not everyone approved of our Sci-Fi Christmas story.

I greeted my family at the end of the play, feeling very proud of my part in the big production. At the exit the Country Girls club members handed out gift bags of candy and nuts to every student. It was the perfect ending to the community event. As we walked along the icy roadway to our car, I clutched my treat bag in one hand and my father's hand in the other. The freezing night air turned our breath into little clouds of mist rising about our faces. Looking up into the shiny blanket of stars and planets overhead, I felt the Christmas Spirit upon me.

Sandra D. Simmer comes from a family of artisans that nurtured her creative spirit. She maintained her interest in the arts while raising a family and pursuing a career in non-profit management. Sandra enjoys traveling and has experienced many interesting travel adventures.

Recently retired to the San Francisco Bay Area, Sandra has followed her love of the written word to write about her colorful life; both real and imagined. She joined several writing groups and credits her mentor friends with expanding her writing skills. Sandra also thanks her children, Erin and Bryce, for their encouragement to take chances with her new writing career.

Sandra is a newly published author with stories in the NCPA's anthologies *Destination: the World Volumes I & II*, and *All Holidays 2020.* She is currently writing her first novel. Sandra can be found on LinkedIn and contacted at sandpiper99@hotmail.com.

PURPLE HEART DAY—MIA

BARBARA KLIDE

P urple Heart Day is celebrated on August 7, which happens to be the day before Dad's birthday. Also on this date, in 1782, George Washington issued the first purple heart—the Badge of Military Merit. It was literally a purple heart-shaped cloth delicately embroidered with the word "MERIT" in the middle, surrounded by sprays of leaves. This military decoration faded from use, but was revived in 1932 as the Purple Heart we know today.

The new medal features George Washington's profile likeness, and is still heart-shaped with a gold border and a shield which was George Washington's coat of arms. The shield is white with three red stars and two red bars between green leaves. It's not quite 1½ inches wide. The ribbon portion is purple, representing the shedding of blood, with two small white strips on either side. The flip side of the medal is a raised bronze heart with the words, "FOR MILITARY MERIT". Over two million Purple Hearts have been awarded to soldiers over the years. Dad was one of them, and he was awarded two.

When we were kids, Dad used to show my brother and me those two medals and my eyes would light up. I loved seeing them sitting on golden velvet inside their own black leather presentation cases embossed with gold trim and the words "Purple Heart". I knew Purple Hearts were given out if a brave soldier was wounded in combat or paid the ultimate sacrifice. Dad once showed us his bullet wound scars near his heart and on his thigh. Years later he gave one of those medals to me and one to his youngest granddaughter, Jessica, for safekeeping.

When I was about 11 or 12, while visiting my paternal grandparents along with my parents and brother, I found myself kid-bored and began snooping through a bedroom nightstand. As I was just closing the drawer, I was caught, severely admonished, and told that I must learn to respect people's privacy. That was after I had already read a Western Union telegram that I'd found inside and had hastily slipped back in.

At first I was perplexed, but the telegram was written in plain English, and after a second read, the message sunk in. Addressed to my grandparents, it read in part, paraphrased, "We are sorry to inform you that your son went missing in action (MIA) and is presumed dead."

I was a shy girl and would not have blurted out questions, especially since I was so embarrassed, but I never forgot it. I left it alone, thinking of it as an adult family secret that no one wished to discuss. The rest of the story was not revealed until some 70 years later when Mom was gone and Dad was in his 90's.

*   *   *

An unofficial military holiday of less than 10 years, National Purple Heart Day does not shut down businesses or banks, but cities, counties, states, Major League Baseball teams, and other veteran and military organizations honor their local medal recipients with events. American flags are flown all over, including at private homes.

There are several Purple Heart groups including the congressionally-chartered veterans' Military Order of the Purple Heart, which offers military and civilian benefits that aid Purple Heart recipient members. One benefit is access to a special license plate with the Purple Heart on it. Dad always had one on his car and he was richly rewarded by having strangers salute him upon noticing it. I can't tell you how heartwarming that was when we drove around together while I was visiting him in Florida.

Some well-known recipients of the Purple Heart include John F Kennedy, who was the only president to receive one, George Patton, Colin Powell, Bob Dole, Kurt Vonnegut, Oliver Stone, Rod Serling, John McCain, and James Garner.

Mom passed in 2004 leaving Dad devastated at the time, but he was a fighter, survivor, and upbeat–and he was mobile, driving wherever he wanted and easily made friends during those years. Growing up a little rough around the edges in the lower east side of Manhattan, he'd lived a long, interesting, and happy life with a loving wife for nearly 60 years. He had adoring kids, grandkids, and his own business which he retired from when he and Mom moved from New York to Florida.

Dad passed on October 10, 2010. He had been diagnosed with terminal pancreatic cancer in February of that year after having surgery to remove a suspicious tumor. He probably had it for some time. That was the beginning of the end.

Immediately following the surgery, Dad was moved to a nursing home near his office on his doctor's advice, from which Dad begged me to rescue him. It was a sad, old facility, and there was minimal effort taken to help the residents beyond basic care. Having been given a death sentence, his wife now gone, and being the only surviving member of his childhood family, Dad appeared to slip into a deep depression with a constant, miserable expression on his face.

He wailed that he was all alone, and it was the only time I had ever heard him say something that left me frightened and feeling helpless, "I want to die, please kill me." I was floored.

Years earlier we had shopped together for private facilities for Mom, and having seen similar nursing homes with urine-smelling halls, we eventually got lucky and found one so close to Mom and Dad's condominium that Dad could see her every day, and he did. The place was acceptable, but had its faults and I was hoping for even better options this time.

I had sworn I would never take Dad to a Veterans Administration (VA) facility because I had heard negative accounts about them, but out of desperation, I decided to call, having been told there was a new facility that was different from the rest. I reached an Admissions Director of the Alexander Nininger Veterans Administration Nursing Home in Pembroke Pines, Florida, and told the director about Dad and his WWII service in the European Theater and that he had full benefits. She said that with full benefits she would be able to put him on the top of a long waiting list to get in and it just so happened that a room opened up that very day. Further, I needed to get down there now and see the place in order for her to hold it. She added that I would be pleasantly surprised.

I dropped everything and rushed there, arriving in time for a tour. After seeing the large, clean-smelling and sunny facility with an enormous aquarium filling one full side of a wall, a floor to ceiling finch enclosure, where the little birds were thriving, and a visiting Golden Retriever therapy dog outfitted in a pink tutu, I wanted to move in myself. Seriously, I was sold. And Dad loved animals.

Within 24 hours I had Dad moved by ambulance to what would become his last home. There, he roomed the first few days with the former editor of the Miami Herald.

Unfortunately, the gentleman had the window bed and kept his curtains closed, keeping the entire room dark. I requested to get Dad into a better room and they accommodated when another one opened. Many aged WWII residents in the facility passed with some frequency. In fact, of the 16 million WWII veterans, less than 100 thousand are still alive with an average of 245 dying every day.

Dad was moved to a room with a window and given a bed facing south, with a view of a green lawn bigger than two soccer fields and a wide open sky where he could see planes take off and come in for a landing from a small airport a few roads away. Dad was a former private pilot, so this was big.

The facility also had a sweet African grey parrot named Congo that we both fell in love with and who seemed to recognize us as we visited him daily. Years later I coincidentally became acquainted with the person who initiated parrot-assisted therapy programs in veteran's facilities across the U.S. With her partner, Dr. Lorin Lindner also started Wolves and Warriors, a TV show on Animal Planet filmed at Lockwood Animal Rescue Center (LARC) which also housed other rescued creatures. They are angels on earth, and as a result, Congo shared a loving home with veterans like Dad.

While writing this story, I decided to see how Congo was doing since I knew that these birds could live 40-60 years under good conditions. Turns out that two years ago, the doctor in the on-site VA pharmacy also fell in love with Congo, and while preparing to retire, asked if he could adopt him and the facility said yes. Congo is now living out his senior years under very good conditions—in his forever home.

The nursing home had the most charming and gregarious activities director, Oscar, who had been a N.Y. Broadway producer and whose singular job was to treat his soldier residents to fun-filled activities both on site and in the community, transporting them with a VA bus equipped to load them while still seated in their wheel chairs. With all of the outside socializing, the veterans had no shortage of people who listened to them, and made them feel they were still important and honored by society.

Wherever you turned, you saw veterans of different wars: World War II (WWII), the Korean War, and the Vietnam War, and they all shared stories at meals, on a couch along the halls, in a large sitting room, out of doors, with the staff, and with visitors. The facility even hosted a few WWI veterans, and it was co-ed, so if you were lucky you might meet some of the amazing women veterans.

*   *   *

During the first few days after arriving, I was invited to a group veterans meeting and was told that this was the only one I would be allowed to attend as they were private and could get extremely emotional. They made this allowance for family members like me when their loved ones are first moved in.

In this group meeting, the Social Services Director Mark

went around the room and asked each veteran why they enlisted. Many had done so immediately after December 7, 1941, when Pearl Harbor was attacked. He also asked what they were grateful for and if there was anything they were looking forward to.

One vet said he joined the army to meet women, which had Dad fuming. Dad passionately and tearfully responded that he joined to protect our country and keep his Ukrainian immigrant parents free. Later we realized that the self-proclaimed Romeo was Dad's new roommate, and I wasn't sure if I needed to intervene, or if Dad would have to make his own peace with him. I caught Dad grumbling under his breath every time the two of them passed each other in the halls while driving their wheel chairs. If serious feelings weren't involved, it would have been funny. However, in the room, the fellow kept the curtains around his bed drawn closed most of the time, which was just fine for both of them.

One soldier in the meeting had been a Prisoner of War (POW) in Germany for 2 years, having lost all his crew when his aircraft was shot down by Nazis. As horrific as his story was, he seemed happy and well-adjusted to his past. This was a guy I wanted Dad to meet and become friends with, so I later wheeled Dad to a veranda where this wonderful soul was gabbing with other happy residents. I knew I'd have to let Dad take over from there and hope the good vibes rubbed off on him.

In that same meeting, Director Mark explained to the group why he included the last two questions. He said the best way to stem depression is to be grateful, something that I could remind Dad of, but had little power to change. The second way is to have something to look forward to—that, I could work with. After arriving a few weeks later back in California where I lived, I began sending Dad fun cards every day. They were doctored up with shiny stickers, faux gems, chipped with sounds, lights, and music. I was told by the receptionist that Dad would wheel himself to the front desk daily to wait for the mail delivery with my cards. It gave him something to look forward to—every day but Sunday. I'm so glad Mark sparked my thinking.

*   *   *

Then it happened. In Dad's private onboarding meeting in Mark's office, that old Western Union telegram finally came full circle.

Dad and I both were very comfortable with this empathetic human being, and having been surrounded by wartime remembrances, Dad started to open up about his. Dad was a raconteur, who I take after; and he began talking about tragic events that he had kept from Mom, my brother and me. He spoke of seeing soldiers freezing cold using gasoline in their helmets to try and keep warm with deadly results. There were other traumatic stories. Dad wept as he went on, eventually launching into the story which led to receiving his first Purple Heart. He was speaking fondly of his brave unit stationed behind enemy lines and one time in particular when they were fired upon. Dad was hit and transported to a portable army hospital. He knew not what happened to his friends.

After surgery, Dad said he was placed on a cot next to another soldier and while getting to know each other, Dad disclosed that he was Jewish. His new pal asked Dad if he knew what German forces would do to him if they found that out. When Dad said he didn't, the soldier told my young, bug-eyed father that he would be used for bayonet practice. To ward against such a fate, he said Dad should permanently discard his U.S. Army dog tags.

When Dad was patched up and sent out to fight again, he took to heart the warning and buried his dog tags somewhere in France. Why? The letter "H" was stamped in the lower righthand corner of his nickel-alloy tags. "H" stood for Hebrew, the religious classification assigned to Jewish servicemen. "H" was not a problem for those fighting the Japanese in the Pacific Theater, but in Europe, the Nazi campaign included the annihilation of Jews, so the prospect of a terrible demise was very real for Dad. However, a different fate was to befall him.

For a second time, Dad was wounded. He was shot

multiple times in the chest and was carried away again, this time far from his unit to some unknown place for medical care, where for many weeks he lay unidentified, having slipped into a coma.

The old U.S. Army telegram erupted from my memory banks and crashed surreally in that office that day. Dad said he eventually regained consciousness and all he could remember of that time was answering a doctor's question, "Who are you?" Dad didn't know he had officially gone missing in action and was presumed dead, nor that the war was over, the troops had begun demobilizing, and were being repatriated from all corners of the globe in a 1945 military project dubbed Operation Magic Carpet.

Can you imagine the shock and joy when his parents got the news that their son was still alive? In retrospect, perhaps my grandparents kept the telegram close at hand to remind them how grateful they were that their beloved son, Everett, made it back home alive.

Dad certainly had something to tell. It just took him seven decades to do so. I couldn't help think that in today's world, a simple DNA test would have brought closure sooner.

Mark concluded the meeting saying that for all these years Dad was suffering from post-traumatic stress disorder (PTSD). As most people know today, it is a mental condition resulting after exposure to one or many traumatic events such as those associated with war and which shares similar symptoms with depression. We knew that Dad also suffered from periodic nightmares, another common symptom, but help was never sought since PTSD treatment wasn't much of a topic for WWII vets, having only been developed in 1980. Mark said he would see to it that Dad got introduced to cognitive behavioral therapy (CBT) to help change his troubling thought patterns.

After we all recovered our composure, Dad shared one more story—one, a hell of a lot cheerier where an MIA soldier safely returns to America from the dead.

Docked not far from the Walter Reed Medical Center, in the District of Columbia, the Andrew Sisters were present to greet the returning soldiers on their ships, including Dad. The Andrew Sisters were instrumental in the war effort and entertained the troops at USO shows around the world. They had a smash hit song called "Boogie Woogie Bugle Boy" that appeared in an Abbott and Costello war movie, which was famously reprised by Bette Midler in 1972, climbing to the Billboard top 10. Great videos for both can be found online.

Patti, the most charismatic of the Andrew Sisters visited Dad at his bedside while he was awaiting release to the med center. As Dad told it, Patti said, "Soldier, besides me, what's the first thing you'd like now that you are back in America?" Dad laughed telling the story and said that he told her that all he really wanted was a chocolate malted milk shake, and Patti, like the Goddess she must have been, delivered.

*   *   *

That day years later in the office of the Social Services Director was exhausting, and ultimately profoundly rewarding. The VA facility had given Dad a link back to his war years with remembrances of the world's unifying fight for freedom. It hooked him up with new friends with a collective history in a phenomenal facility, and gave him another reason to be content with his life and his commitment as an American warrior. And he was damn proud of his two Purple Hearts.

Over the next few months, my brother, Robert, and his family flew in from NY and Dad got to meet his new great granddaughter, Erica, the only one he would meet of several "greats" to come. Friends also dropped in, and Dad's frozen heart slowly thawed and reopened to how grateful he truly was for having these loved ones in his life, and the many visits he had to look forward to. He had returned to his happier self.

*   *   *

Before I went home to California, I got the bright idea of giving Dad a Hallmark correspondence box with a combined total of 53 postcards and letter stationery. On the address side of every one of them, I affixed a 44 cent Purple Heart stamp, the first class postage rate at the time, and his new VA home address label. I provided him with pre-printed mailing labels in duplicate for all his family and friends so he merely had to peel off the one for the person he wanted to write to and stick it on his choice of stationery. I included booklets of colorful stickers so he could dress them up as I had done on my daily cards to him. The box turned out to be a lifeline, and a beloved nephew of his told me that he teared up after receiving one such letter from Dad, and would treasure it.

Months later when Dad was in hospice, I showed him the box, and asked if he might like to dictate any more messages that I could help him write. He slowly touched the box and with opaque eyes, and a barely detectable smile, silently shook his head no.

I had sent Dad a chipped greeting card, with fireflies still blinking on it, that he was buried with, a symbol of "shining from the inside out"—it fit. He also had his cap from the 82nd Airborne, his U.S. Army infantry division. We laid Dad to rest next to Mom in the Star of David cemetary in Florida.

There was no place I would rather have been in those days than there with Dad. I was his loving daughter, and he and Mom will always be alive and well in my heart.

* * *

After Dad passed, I counted a total of only 11 cards and letters remaining, from over four dozen, in his stationery box. Dad said his last words to his loved ones in writing– each one stamped in the upper righthand corner with the Purple Heart.

If you use social media you may wish to use the hashtag #PurpleHeartDay on Instagram on August 7, and show your support of the courage and devotion of American patriots who have served.

Barbara Klide was born in NYC. She is the author of the book trilogy, *Along Came Ryan...the Little Gosling King*, the true saga of a mated pair of elegant, sensitive and smart Canada geese and their offspring who nested three years in a row where she works. She donates book profits to various wildlife rescue groups.

She also has published short stories in the NCPA Anthology series of books.

Barbara graduated with an MBA from Golden Gate University, San Francisco, and a Certificate in Graphic Design from the University of California, Davis. She is the Director of Marketing for Quest Technology Management, California and a member of the NCPA. Her Canada goose compendium series has received much acclaim including from Dr. Lorin Lindner, PhD, *Wolves and Warriors*, as seen on Animal Planet and Bill Bianco, President, Audubon Society, Sacramento.

Barbara and her longtime partner, reside in Fair Oaks, California where they rescue, foster, and adopt out cats. Visit Barbara at: Barbaraklide.com

Northern California
publishers & authors

NCPA * OUR PURPOSE * WHO WE ARE * WHAT WE DO

Northern California Publishers & Authors (NCPA) is an alliance of independent publishers, authors, and publishing professionals in Northern California.

Formed in 1991 as Sacramento Publishers Association, then expanded to Sacramento Publishers and Authors and eventually to NCPA, our purpose is to foster, encourage, and educate authors, small publishers, and those interested in becoming authors and publishers.

Service providers who cater to the publishing industry – illustrators, cover designers, editors, etc. – are also invited to join NCPA as associate members.

We support small indie presses, self-publishers and aspiring authors at our monthly meetings by covering topics such as self- and traditional publishing, editing, book design, author-related tax and legal issues, and marketing.

In addition to our annual NCPA Book Anthology, for *members only*, which started again in 2019, NCPA holds an annual Book Awards Competition for both *members, and non-members*. The NCPA Book Awards Competition celebrated our 27th year in 2021 with the entry of 36 books published in 2020.

NCPA has also given back to the community through proceeds from a Silent Auction during our Book Awards Banquets in the forms of: $1000 scholarship to a college-bound, local high school senior intending to pursue a publishing or writing-related degree; 916-Ink, which empowers youth through the published, written word; Mustard Seed School for underprivileged youth. This year all proceeds will go to Friends of the Sacramento Public Library, which provides books to the homes of underprivileged children.

Check out our website www.norcalpa.org for information on our next Book Awards Competition, the next anthology and information on how to join NCPA.

Due to the 2020 pandemic, monthly meetings were temporarily moved to Zoom. When the quarantine lifted, we changed to hybrid meetings by resuming in-person, plus maintaining our Zoom meetings. For current information on our meetings, contact www.norcalpa.org

OTHER NCPA ANTHOLOGIES

Purchase anthologies at Amazon, Samati Press, or in person from any author in the Holiday Anthology. Anthologies are also available in eBook format. Information on each author in all anthologies can be found on the NCPA website: www.norcalpa.org.

BIRDS OF A FEATHER

An NCPA Anthology

A Collection of Short Stories about Animals

From their size, color, and the way they see the world, animals are diverse—and so are the delightful stories in this anthology. Ranging from legends and true tales of wildland bears to a memorable veterinary house call and stories of humans who become animals (or act like them), this collection is all about animals and our relationships with them. Meet rabbits, lizards, guinea pigs, potbelly pigs, horses, seals, owls, spiders, coyotes, wolves, elephants, and of course plenty of cats and dogs who will touch your heart and remind you that no matter how many legs we have, we all have much in common.

MORE BIRDS OF A FEATHER
An NCPA ANTHOLOGY
A Collection of Short Stories about Animals and Other Things

Within these pages are thirty non-fiction stories—some happy, some sad; some exciting, some glad; some daring, some caring—about a variety of animals. Add a little fiction: one far-out adventure and one fantasy, and toss in a couple of on-going series, previously introduced in *Birds of a Feather*.

There's Nacht, our resident feral cat who presents Tux, then our fun shape-shifters Dex and Felicity as the red fox and Arctic fox. Meet two elk and three penguins; a bunny that wouldn't give up; two elephants; a goat on the run; a potty-trained pig; two squirrels; and a bunch of wild birds, including a gosling, plus tame chickens: Lady Cluck and her girls; lizards in the Caribbean; crickets; a gorilla; a bear; a tortoise; and a variety of cats and dogs.

And a partridge in a pear tree? Maybe not, but the second NCPA anthology from 2019 is a lot of chirping fun.

Take a journey around the world with 35 authors from NCPA as they share their stories covering nearly every continent and a vast array of cultures. This collection of charming and endearing tales will take you on excursions beyond your own backyard from breathtaking trips of a lifetime to harrowing adventures and comical misadventures.

Enjoy more than thirty non-fiction stories, including: A Long-awaited Trip to Greece * "Wogging" in Ireland * China by Train * Ghosts in BC * and a First-Time Flight from Nigeria to America. If you're looking for fiction, discover the secret behind *Lance's Toboggan of Miracles,* follow the further adventures of Knacht, the Wanderer who stops wandering, and continue the fantasy adventures of our favorite shape-shifters, Dex and Felicity (introduced in NCPA's 2019 anthologies: *Birds of a Feather* and *More Birds of a Feather*), as they take their romance on the road with a honeymoon in Hawaii.

Enjoy more than thirty stories, including: the Loma Prieta earthquake; a missing earring in Williamsburg, VA; a trip to Havana, Cuba; a mistaken identity in Italy; the Nigeria-Biafra Civil War; a search for weapons in Israel; and a near arrest in Italy. Immerse yourself in this diverse, one-of-a-kind NCPA Anthology.

In addition, this volume features the 4th fantasy installment of the red Fox and the Great Horned Owl, our favorite shape-shifters, Dex and Felicity as they meet the Menehune's in Hawaii, and the 4th installment of Nacht, the feral cat, and his adventures. Let your heart be warmed when Nacht meets his forever human on the canals of Venice.

This *Destination: The World, Volume Two*, covers it all from A to Z: America to Zimbabwe, and everywhere in-between. There's a story within these pages for everyone.

Our cover indicates winter holidays, but NCPA offers this warning: "Don't Judge a Book by its Cover". ALL Holidays means exactly that, ALL HOLIDAYS. NCPA's 1st Annual ALL Holiday 2020 anthology includes a variety of traditional and non-traditional holidays from New Year's Day to New Year's Eve, with celebrations from many lands, religions, and cultures. And for the first time we introduce poetry in all forms: from rhyming and free form, to traditional and non-traditional Haiku, plus Haikai, Haibun, Renga and Cherita.

We look forward to a Christmas return of two favorites: our shapeshifter foxes, Dex and Felicity with a new romantic adventure, and reforming-feral cat, Nacht, tells a new batch of ferals a fireside story. There's even a taste of some of the wild and goofy national holidays that are celebrated each month.

NCPA's First Holiday Anthology is packed as full as a Christmas stocking with enjoyable stories and entertaining traditions.